Folly at Sausmarez Manor

Majestic Estates Series, Volume 0

IreAnne Chambers

Published by Purple Storm Publishing, 2018.

This is a work of fiction. Similarities to real people, places, or events are entirely coincidental.

FOLLY AT SAUSMAREZ MANOR

First edition. December 6, 2018.

Copyright © 2018 IreAnne Chambers.

ISBN: 979-8227638069

Written by IreAnne Chambers.

Table of Contents

DEDICATION

To the family I love and my best friends of forever.

THE FOLLY BEGINS

When chivalry and folly collide, can true love be far behind?

The last thing Lady Cordelia Rutledge expected to find during her family visit to Guernsey Island was a husband. But when an innocent tour of the island finds her stranded, unchaperoned, with her charming guide, an arranged marriage seems imminent as the only way to satisfy her family and salvage her reputation. So much for her tour of the continent...

If archaeologist Marshall Compton, Marquess of Daventry, had known his chivalrous offer to act as the lovely Cordelia's guide would land him a fiancée, he probably wouldn't have made it in the first place. The only thing he knows for certain, however, is that his plans for an Indian expedition are most assuredly lost.

But before Cordelia and Marshall can embark on a future together, they must contend with an ancient cult, run-ins with the Russians (or are they pirates?), and the mystical secrets hidden in Guernsey folklore—all while managing the ultimate folly... falling in love.

AUTHOR'S NOTE

Some artistic license is used to fictionalize the setting and story lines relative to the Island of Guernsey in 1801, Sausmarez Manor, and island folklore. Any discrepancies between fact, fiction, and folklore with regard to the majestic home of Sausmarez Manor and Guernsey Island is intentional and used strictly for this work of fiction and for the enjoyment of my readers.

The characters and events portrayed in this book are fictitious or are used fictitiously. Any similarity to real persons, living or dead, is purely coincidental and not intended by the author. Pivotal dates in history, places, and relevant historical figures may be mentioned or make cameo appearances, but the details associated with these dates, places, and people as they pertain to the story are a work of fiction for the enjoyment of my readers and not intended to portray actual events in history.

Care has been taken to avoid dialogue/narrative that may be considered offensive to some readers in modern times. However, please know the words and thoughts in this book are portrayed by characters in the time of 1801. Any use or perceived use of any such offensive dialogue/narrative does not reflect specific viewpoints of the author, but may be used very minimally to create historically accurate content. It is not the intention of the author to promote or condone anything that may be considered offensive in modern times.

CHAPTER ONE

Guernsey Island - Dehus Dolmen
October 1801

"What do you mean we are locked in?" The high-pitched squeal of distress echoes in the dampness.

Lord Marshall Compton, Marquess of Daventry surveys the passage. "Someone has blocked the entrance." Marshall's willowy fingers creep along the stone edges of the darkened tomb like the long legs of a spider, searching for any small opening. At least their lamps remain lit, and they're not in total darkness.

"You mean we're trapped in here? In the tomb of— with mummies?" Short breaths spurt out between her lips. "How will we ever survive the night? Is there enough air? What will happen once we are discovered! My lord, I cannot endure a scandal." Hiccups come next. Lady Cordelia Rutledge is close to panic. No, it *is* panic. One more hiccup and surely she will faint.

Marshall puts his lamp on the ground, grabs her arms, and turns her to face him. Ice-blue eyes glare back. Strands of apricot-colored hair dangle about her cheeks.

Those eyes glaze over. He shakes her with each word from his mouth. "Please. Calm yourself."

Silence. His gloved hands rub up and down her arms to will her the courage to be strong. "We will get out, my lady, I assure you." Her pale white face stares past him at the stone closure that seals them in. Truth be told, he isn't sure if his men will find them. Most important at this point? Keep her calm. He cannot endure a panic-stricken female.

Lady Delia's eyes narrow. Anger replaces hysteria. A deep and pointed monotone sound follows. No high-pitched squeal. The muscles in her arms tighten. "And to be locked in with the likes of you, no less." Her fists grind hard against his chest. Marshall grabs her wrists and holds them tight between them until her struggle subsides. There. That's better.

He lowers his voice. Maybe that will get her to lower hers. "I understand your concerns. I assure you there will be no scandal. I left word at Havilland's I would return before nightfall. My people will be out to find us." Marshall relaxes his hold and releases one of her arms. He places his palm in the small of her back and guides her gently to a stone bench against the wall. The light from the lamp he placed on the floor flickers slightly but is still full flame. A good sign.

Lady Delia remains rattled. Her anger, too, is waning. Her countenance relaxes, and her voice is less shrill. "Why, pray tell, would they not consider you had changed your mind and decided to stay out? Is that not the custom of gentlemen? What makes you think they will not relish the notion of you ruining me? I'm not supposed to be here. They'll see we're alone."

"First, I can assure you, it's not *my* custom." He's certainly not discussing it with her. "Second, I can see you are not up on the local tales. And third, my people are loyal and vetted. I have procedures in place. If I intend to stay out all night, they are informed." Will she see through his attempt to keep her in check? The lines on her forehead crimp for a moment while she sits. Silence again.

She smooths her pelisse and clears her throat. "I assure you, I do not need to be up on local tales to know what happens when a lady is found alone with a gentleman for any amount of time, but you must know to be found alone in a place such as this is unheard of!" Lady Delia pulls at the wrist of each of her kid gloves, flexing her fingers to adjust the fit.

Maybe if he redirects? "Yes, and allow me to enlighten you. The Guernsey locals fear the spell casters who are said to converge at night at their meeting place, the Catioroc, between L'Eree and Perelle."

"Spell casters! Certainly you do not give merit to such balderdash, not to mention the fact that the Catioroc is much farther south of where we are anyway." Lady Delia sits up straight. Her voice wavers. "I do not give such inclinations any credence." She splays her fingers wide to adjust the fit of her gloves once again.

"So you know of the Catioroc, do you? I wasn't aware you were familiar with the area."

"My lord, I may only have been here a couple of weeks, but I have become quite familiar with where we are on this island. The prehistoric ruins fascinate me. I have taken it upon myself to know my surroundings."

Marshall watches. He ignores the niggle in his brain when she talks of her interest in ruins. This particular conversation will have to wait. He must find a way to get them out. Her hands remain folded in her lap. Probably a good sign. "Whether you or I believe or not, the locals do. Since you have taken it upon yourself to know your surroundings, have you not seen them all with their witches' seats in front of their houses?"

"Witches' seats? I have never heard such nonsense." Lady Delia pats down each side of her hair and tugs each glove one more time. Maybe not good after all.

Even in the lamplight, Marshall can see the pale of her skin and the tremble of her chin. This line of conversation must stop, at least for the moment, or until they find their way out of this tomb. What was he thinking bringing her here? Of all the places on Guernsey Island to show her. He wasn't. "Nonsense or not, it is what they believe." Warm air suffocates his lungs. His breaths are short, and his mind is racing faster than Aladdin's magic carpet.

Attempts to leave the conversation are in vain. "Surely, you do not believe in spell casters?"

"It doesn't matter what I believe, although there is a witches' seat in the front garden of Havilland Hall. So they cannot have any grievance with me. Or you, for that matter, since you are with me."

Lady Delia ignores his efforts to mollify her fears. "And for what purpose is this done, pray tell?" More fidgeting with the blasted gloves.

"To give the witches' a place to rest, of course!" Marshall breaths in deep and studies her reaction. "It's thought safer to be kind to them and give them a place to rest outside of the home rather than have them wreak havoc."

"I don't understand the reasonings of such ones." Lady Delia removes the offensive gloves one delicate finger at a time. She fans her forehead and presses the back of her hand against it.

The lamplight flickers but continues to burn. At least she doesn't know he suspects the stone bench they're sitting on is a tomb. Wicked thoughts of walking dead pulsing their way in pursuit of their prize cause him to smile. One smile he immediately regrets.

Lady Delia holds up her gloves in defense. "I am not loose." She fans her face and almost hits his chin. "I cannot help it. The air is hot and heavy. I can't breathe. Removing my gloves seems of least concern."

Marshall can't disagree.

More fanning, more sighing. "If this continues, I don't know what we shall do."

More wicked thoughts invade his senses. What the devil is the matter with him? Redheaded females trekking the island alone in search of prehistoric remnants is what. He should have left her to her own designs.

This discourse must move in a different direction. For the moment. "Surely local legend is not too absurd for you. Your own Scottish heritage speaks of similar beliefs, does it not?"

"I suppose it does, but one does not continue believing in such nonsense in this age. You must see the ridiculousness of it."

"Being that my interests surround archeology and studies of the past, ridiculous or not, those who believe in such things, believe in them strongly and, as such, fear them strongly. That is what gives those beliefs strength whether we believe it or not."

"I see some truth in your words. I, on the other hand, prefer to remain firm that such is utter nonsense."

"Around here, my lady, you may want to keep those beliefs to yourself."

"Maybe it was a spell caster that locked us in here." Humor in her eyes mocks him.

Tease her. That's what he'll do. "Best not to jest, for it may have been the local fairies that closed us in." Better this way than all-out war with a pair of kid gloves.

"Fairies?" That rewards him with a half-smile. Much better than panic.

"Yes, fairies. In Scotland, I believe they're called brownies."

"Hmm...brownies. I remember hearing tales about brownies from my nursemaid."

"Yes, and that tale will have to wait for tomorrow... I think I hear something." Marshall reaches for the lantern, stands up, and lifts it up above his head as he walks near where the sounds are coming from. *Scratch, scratch, scratch. Tsak, tsak.* Someone or some*thing* is clawing at the outer side of the stone wall.

Marshall's voice is blunted by stone. "Hello! We're in here! Can you hear me?" *Scratch, scratch, scratch. Tsak, tsak.* Methodical clanks of metal to stone and crumbling dirt continue. No response. Are they digging them out? Or God forbid—sealing them in?

Lady Delia adds to an excited ensemble. Will their voices together elicit some acknowledgment from the other side of the stone barrier?

Scratch, scratch, scratch. Tsak, tsak...

"Aah-oooooh! Aah-aah, aah-oooooh!"

"What is that?" The sound is close. Just outside the stones. The scratching and scraping doesn't stop either. Lord Daventry doesn't answer. Only stands and stares. Is he even listening? Delia reaches out to touch his arm, and he swings around and shoves her behind him.

"You need to stand back."

"For what? Who's out there? Do you know who's getting us out of here?"

"Yes."

"Excellent." The fear bending through her body begins to straighten. "You're a man of your word, and your people *are* loyal to you. They've come for us." Delia angles forward to look around him. Lord Daventry turns to face her.

Shadows blacken his already dark features. What's wrong with him? It's almost... Is he afraid? "I know it must be my men, but I have to warn you."

"Warn me? About what?"

"Aah-oooooh! Aah-aah, aah-oooooh!" *Scratch, scratch, scratch. Tsak, tsak.*

"That!" Lord Daventry's tone changes to rigid.

"What is *that*?"

"You really have no idea?" He slides his fingers through his dark hair. Thick, wavy, dark hair.

Dirt and rocks fall in and roll toward Delia's feet. Happy gushes press through what was addled panic moments ago. Freedom is imminent. Relief. At last. Beads of sweat line Lord Daventry's forehead. "My lord, what's the matter?"

"Listen. It's very important that when the way is clear, you stay very close to me. Do you understand?"

Of all the rakish schemes. What thick-witted inclination possessed her to accompany him when he asked? "If you think to try and make this out to be more than what it is, now that we may try to get out of here with no scandal—" If only the sight of the man didn't make her insides want to buckle...

"What? No! You must listen to me. I'm only trying to keep you safe."

"If you will only tell me what it is."

A large mound of dust and dirt puffs into the air and an oblong opening appears. Fresh air begins to cool the space before scrabbling sounds and muffled words follow.

"Behind me! Now, my lady!" Lord Daventry doesn't wait for her to react. He shoves her behind him again before she can protest. The light from the lantern wobbles her vision. Almond-shaped eyes move in from the outside. Floating. Floating toward them in the darkness. Lips smack. Whines and sniffs follow.

Delia's heart pounds in her chest. The muscles of Lord Daventry's back tense. She leans against him for support. Can he feel the fear grip her?

The whine stops, and the animal stands directly in front of them. Delia is afraid to look. She presses her face to Lord Daventry's shoulder. Forget scandal. She presses her entire body against him. He breaks the silence.

"Hey boy, easy...easy...?"

"Hey boy?" She steps back from Lord Daventry at the same time the animal lunges, putting its front two paws on the marquess' shoulders and knocking him to the ground. The length of its body is covered in matted, black fur. Lord Daventry is stock still, except for his lips. "Lady Delia. Do. Not. Move."

The animal doesn't like that command. It glares right at her. She doesn't falter. It turns back to Daventry and proceeds to claim ownership of him. Wet dog kisses. Not what she expects from this overgrown mongrel. Not moving is no longer an option. She doubles over. Her laughter turns to a cough because of the dust still floating in the air.

Lord Daventry can't move. "My lady, this animal is not predictable." He waves her to stop. "You must contain yourself immediately."

"I'm sorry, my lord. But do you know how absolutely ridiculous you look, lying there pinned to the ground by two paws of an oversize mutt-breed?" The dog proceeds to flop on top of him and glare almond-shaped eyes at her.

"I'm telling you, he may appear playful, but he's not. I've seen this dog maul a man. Few on the island are not afraid of him."

"How is it that he is still around? I mean if he's that dangerous, how did your men work while he was outside with them?

"We shall soon find out I hope. I'll need to get him to let me up so I can talk to someone out there." Lord Daventry tries to sit up. The weight of the animal holds him down.

"Let me try. What do you call him?"

"I don't call him anything."

"What do you mean? He's not yours?"

"Mine? No."

"He acts like he's yours. He's obviously protective of you."

"He came on the same boat with me when I sailed to the Island. He was much smaller then. I shared my food with him on the boat, and when we got here, he followed me around a few days but then took off on his own." Maybe this man is not the rake he appears to be. "He's wild and lives in the woods. The locals think he's some kind of protector. Only likes certain people. Others, he just will not embrace. Very dangerous animal if he chooses against you."

"And you were afraid he wouldn't like me?" Knots and braids of worry begin to wind around Delia like a frenzied coiffure.

"Like I said, I've seen him maul a man. I don't know who he will like and who he will not. And I don't know what makes him threatened."

"I've been told it has to do with whether or not you're afraid. Dogs know. I'm just going to go over there to the entrance and try to talk to someone."

"Lady Delia, no. Please. Wait."

"We can't stay here all night. He's perfectly content there with you. If he was going to attack me, he would have."

Lord Daventry's deep breaths raise the animal on top of his chest. "Move slowly."

Delia walks toward the entrance. She ignores the knotted mess inside. Ignores fear. Swallows hard. She's not afraid. Animal eyes rove in sync with her movements. She bends down to see through the space the dog crawled through. Motion and hubbub. Nothing else.

"Hello? Can you hear me?" She wags her arm around in the space to get their attention.

"Hello? Miss?" A bent knee appears first, then a sideways face peers back through the small, darkened opening.

"Yes, I'm sealed in here with Lord Daventry and that animal, the one that just crawled through."

"Is Lord Daventry all right? Sorry about the dog, my lady. Nothing we could do. He would not be held back. It was him that found you. Good thing, too, because we were looking in the wrong place."

Delia looks back at the dog sprawled full body on top of the marquess. Content. This dog *must* be their protector, not executioner. She turns back to the entrance.

"So how are we to get out of here?"

"It looks as though you might have to crawl out the way the dog crawled in."

"What? How in God's name are we supposed to do that?"

"I believe we can help pull you through. You'll need to come head first. You can see the dog is enormous. If he can come through, you should fit the same. The stones are heavy, we can't move them. You'll have to try."

Delia's heart races. What if she gets stuck? The air inside is too warm.

The dog yawns behind her. "What are they saying? I can't hear them." Lord Daventry's voice is as raspy as a frightened cat. The weight of the dog must be stifling him.

"They want us to crawl out the way the dog came in. The stones are too heavy to move."

"I feared as much. No choice. Go first, I'll follow."

"Will he let you?"

"Don't worry. You must go first. I would suggest removing your outer garments. It's a tight space. You'll need to be free of obstruction to insure you fit easily."

"Remove my what?" He is a rake! "I will not!"

A low growl grumbles from the dark mound planted on Lord Daventry's chest.

CHAPTER TWO

Muffled sounds of fabric whoosh in Marshall's ears. "Are you sure you don't need assistance?"

"No, I do not need assistance." Another whoosh passes above him. "And keep your eyes closed." He can't help it. He peeks. The dim light of the man-made cave doesn't cooperate. All he sees are shadows. "And your face in the other direction. It's not as if you could assist in your present state anyway." True. "That animal has not moved once other than to voice his opinions. Why don't you just shove him off you?"

"Arrruf! Arrruf!" The beast's claws clamp down into Marshall's ribcage. It's Lady Delia's tone. She doesn't understand this animal is more than a large dog. This one is different. She needs to get out of this tomb. Only then can he deal with this mongrel himself. He tries to shift, but the pain in his side stabs pulses through his abdomen. He turns to look. Lady Delia is crouched down with her back against the tomb wall, clutching her undergarments in her hand. *Undergarments?* Of course. That might work. Hopefully, it removes enough bulk to get her through the opening. What is she waiting for?

"My lady. You need to move."

"I don't think I can. He won't stop staring at me."

"I think it's safe to say he wants me to stay and you to go. Just do it slow and cautious."

"What about you? How are you going to get out?"

"Don't worry about me. We'll get to that after you are safe and back home. Instruct the men to get you to Sausmarez. I'll come later. It is best we're not seen returning together."

Lady Delia continues to sit on the dirt floor, still not budging. The voice from outside yells in again.

"Are you about ready to come through, m'lady?"

Marshall needs to get her to focus without disturbing his highness sitting on his chest. "Lady Delia?" He tries not to raise his voice too high. "Come, you must hurry. It's time to get out of here." Her eyes catch his for seconds in time before she shoves the cream-colored cloth she's holding to the side, balls herself onto all fours, and crawls toward the opening.

"This is absurd. I can't believe we are being dictated to by an oversize *dog*."

"Arrruf!" That garners him additional stabs in the ribcage. It's good the dog's enormous pads are clutched at his ribs and not somewhere else, or there would be two males yowling. God only knows what the animal would do then.

"Lady Delia! Please, we need to get out the safest way we can. This is it. Don't delay any longer."

"I don't know how this is going to work." She crouches down to look through the opening. "I can't even see anymore. It's dark!"

"Doesn't matter. The wall is not very thick. You can do it."

"And what if there are 'things' in there?"

"What *things*?"

"I don't know, insects or crawly things?"

"There are no insects or crawly things. It is stone."

"But there's dirt on the bottom where it was dug through."

"My lady, have you forgotten where we are? Would you rather stay in here?"

"No, of course not. I am just not delighted about crawling through there!"

"My lady, you must do it."

She raises up on her knees and flails her hands in the air. "I know. I know."

"Don't think about it. Think only of getting out."

Marshall watches and waits. The mutt licks his lips and begins to pant. Her head ducks down in the opening first then her elbows folded under her chest. Her body wiggles ahead to the right and then the left until the only thing visible are her legs and boots. All movement stops.

Delia wiggles left then right to try to squeeze through the opening. Elbows tight against her sides, she maneuvers forward. The cold stone scratches against her cheeks. Her eyes squint shut. No creepy crawlies. Hair tickles her forehead. The other side of the opening appears, revealing a clear, dark sky widening out. A deep breath wedges itself in her chest. Men walk in one direction then the other. Where did they all come from? Their words form, but to understand them proves beyond her comprehension. Russians! They must be Russians! Why are they here? Why now? Discretion is hardly possible now.

"My lady, come, let us assist you further." Delia's arms are cemented to her sides. She attempts to dislodge one side or the other. Nothing.

"Try to relax, my lady."

"Relax? I can barely breath. I'm suffocating!"

"No, you're not. There is plenty of air."

"Don't tell me I'm not, for I can't inhale!" Pain in her side mounts. "With all these men, can no one move a bloody stone?"

"Calm yourself, you must try to be calm. I assure you, we will loosen it."

"Oh, fiddle. I can't breathe I tell you!" Her head pounds. What is this man going on about? She tries to look up at the activity bristling about her before pinpoint stars pull at the edge of her vision. Her head drops. Blackness darker than the tomb foams before her eyes.

Marshall lifts his head from the ground. The oversize beast finally raises himself up and off to sniff where Lady Delia's feet are not moving. Marshall curls himself to all fours and crawls toward her. "My lady!" He reaches for her feet to shake them. Nothing. "Lady Delia!" Still Nothing. "Hello? Who's out there?"

"Arrruf! Arrruf!"

Marshall glares at the animal. Forget fear. The lady is no longer in danger of this varmint. "You think you can be heard over me?"

"Arrruf! Arrruf!"

"Hello? Someone? Answer me!" Movement above Lady Delia's limbs forces him to fall back on his heels. Stone is shifting above her. Pebbles and gravel split, crumble, and roll off her to land in front of him. He raises his arm across his forehead. He coughs from the dust clogging the chamber.

What the devil are they doing? The large stone shifts above Lady Delia. They're going to cause the entire structure to collapse! Instead, her body is pulled straight through the opening. At least she is out.

"My lord! Can you hear me?" Clear, black darkness replaces the space where she lay.

Marshall bends forward. "Ozanne! Is that you?"

"Yes, my lord. Can you make your way out now that we've been able to open the entrance wider?"

Marshall doesn't respond. He crawls through. He needs to find out what happened to Lady Delia. Is she okay? He hasn't heard one sound from her mouth. Who are all these men?

Marshall stands up, wipes the dirt off, and visually inspects his surroundings. "Ozanne, where did they all come from?"

"I don't know, my lord. We came according to your instructions for such instances when you've not returned as planned. They were here. Apparently, they're Russians."

"But, *why* are they here? This far north? The Russians are in St. Peter Port and Alderney. Are you sure they're Russians?"

"They are dressed like Russians, my lord, are they not? They speak with an accent. Could they be moving down from Alderney? Perhaps to disembark?"

"Yes, I had heard they were preparing for departure. Although, I thought it already occurred. I suppose it's possible. But I cannot believe they would be moving now. This late."

"I'm sorry, sir. I didn't question their help getting the stone moved. If they hadn't stepped up to make the stake we used as a lever to maneuver the stones, we might not have had you out so soon."

"Yes, yes. Quite right. I should be thankful for their help. Do you know who's in charge? I must thank them appropriately."

"Can't say as I got that far. The lady worked herself in a panic, and we had to get her out. Pulled her out myself, as she passed out before we got the stone moved."

"Where is Lady Cordelia?" Marshall spins around to find her.

"We sent her to a cottage not far from here where my sister and her family reside. I thought it best not to have her go back with you given these unfortunate circumstances. She'll need rest after such trauma, I'm sure. No doubt an apothecary might need to be called."

Marshall slaps Ozanne on the back. "Good thinking. Best do what we can to avoid scandal."

Marshall surveys the men milling around a campfire. They've put up for the night. Torches are strategically placed around the area. No, they don't look like Russians. What do Russians look like? "Which one is giving the orders?"

"That one. There." Ozanne motions in the direction of a man leaning against the tomb. His hair is unkempt and long around his ears and collar. His eyes are dark. Midnight dark and sunk in his face. Marshall watches him. There is a firm set to his jaw. A stiffness to his stance. This one's dress is cleaner than those around the fire. They serve him, no doubt. He's the "master" of these serfs. He stares in the fire and sips from a tin cup held with one hand. His glare shifts to peer over the cup. He locks eyes with Marshall. He raises his cup to him, a silent salute. An invitation.

Marshall accepts. He walks toward him. Ozanne yells from behind.

"Lord Daventry, if I may?"

Marshall turns sideways to Ozanne. "What is it?"

"It's Lady Cordelia."

"What about her?"

"There's a problem." Ozanne pulls at the sleeve of a man standing next to him to bring him forward. "This is William and his wife." The woman curtsies. The man bows. "My sister's servants. Sent to collect her to the cottage."

"What are you saying?" Marshall turns all the way around now and jogs back to his steward.

"I'm saying I don't know who took the Miss or where they took her."

"What! How did this happen? Don't you know your own sister's servants?"

"Of course, my lord. They said they were hired only last week."

"And you believed them?"

"Sir, there was no reason not to. With all the confusion to get you out, I—"

Marshall raises his hand. "We'll discuss this later. What direction did they go?" Marshall looks over his shoulder at the Russian overlord who has now joined his men at the fire.

"Can't say as I know, sir. I handed her to those I thought were sent by my sister then swent back to help get you, my lord."

Acid churns Marshall's stomach. Did someone seal them in on purpose? No time to contemplate the reasons now. He must find her. Four directions of roads lead out from the tomb. It's unlikely they took the direction behind it. It's blocked by the

Russians and the tomb. Not easily accessible with a cart. That leaves three.

"Ozanne, take a torch and look for track marks."

Marshall grabs another torch and runs in the opposite direction. The Russians watch. The overlord watches. Two of the roads show signs of travel by cart.

"Ozanne! What have you found?"

"Nothing over here, my lord!"

Good. At least only two directions will need to be scouted. Both lead to the Braye du Valle. It's high tide. He doesn't want to think of what might happen if they take her to the water.

"Ozanne, take William and follow the direction to the west. Send a messenger to her family with word of what has happened. I'll go south toward Vale Castle."

Ozanne runs and calls for the carts brought by the servants from Marshall's house.

The overlord walks over to where Marshall is giving orders. "The lady was taken that way."

West. Marshall's gut calls out "warning." Something isn't right. "Are you sure?"

Master overlord doesn't answer. He sips from his tin cup and returns to his place at the fire.

Marshall watches the Russians and their master. He can't let it rest. He doesn't trust them. What are they doing here?

"Shall we await the mutt?"

"What?" Marshall leers back at Ozanne, who rolls up beside him and hops off.

"The mutt. Do you want him along?"

"No. He takes care of himself. Did he follow me out of that blasted dolmen?" Marshall hands his torch to a servant, steps up on the seat, and grabs hold of the reins. The second cart is brought near, and Ozanne changes places with the driver.

"I believe so, yes. Took off down the road there." Ozanne waves in the direction of Vale Castle.

Ozanne heads west while Marshall surveys the area one last time to locate the cur. Nowhere. "I wonder."

CHAPTER THREE

"Be still my lady."

The female voice speaking above her is soft. Delia's head hurts. She tries to lift her arm and even it hurts. The weight of it pulls back down toward the ground. Sharp stabs sear through the sinews of her arm. She lay flat on her back, jostling back and forth. Where is she? She opens her eyes, but it's dark. She breathes in cold, black night air. The woman next to her holds a lantern swaying back and forth. Her round, white face scrunches sour in the middle. She hovers over Delia's face. The woman's gray tresses hang long on each side of her shoulders. The ends tickle Delia's cheeks.

"We'll have to wait for the healer to tell us for sure, but I'd say you've nothing a good night's rest won't cure."

Healer? Delia's words will not come out. Events in the tomb revisit her. Where is Lord Daventry? Where are they taking her? What of that dratted animal—dog? No one can know she was alone in the tomb with Daventry. Delia's words still will not come out. What is wrong? Her brain is speaking, but her mouth is not willing. Wet tears swell and blur her vision. She stares hard at the woman sitting next to her.

"There, there, my lady. Don't worry. We'll take good care of you. The master gave his instructions. It won't be too long before we're home." A hand pats her arm. "You'll not need to worry yourself." A blanket is pulled to her chin. Warm. Cool fingers smooth her hair back off her face. What's the point? Who will see her hair in the dark?

Relief. Delia cries for relief. Wants to speak out. Wants to thank her or thank Lord Daventry, but nothing will move in her mouth. Home. A warm bed and soft, fluffy blankets. Soothing and nourishing. To whose home are they taking her? Sausmarez? What will people say? Quiet cries clamor and bear down on her heart. She turns her head to the side and closes her eyes. The cart's shuffle shakes her wobbly flesh. Darkness overwhelms the air. Dim waves of glow from the lantern, hanging on a pole attached to the cart, emit faint flickers. Shadows outline the edges. What is wrong with her? What was it Lord Daventry spoke to her about? Brownies? Nonsense.

Empty. The cart is empty. Marshall holds the lantern above his head and walks around it. Why would they leave it here? Obviously intentional since they untethered the horses. Red wheels stand out against the blue color of the body. The gold trim is odd. And the symbol painted on the rear. Some form of a Celtic knot with tints of blue and green leaf designs. Does it stand for something? It's too prominent not to.

Marshall kneels and inspects the tracks. He follows the line all the way to the edge of the Braye. He walks back to the cart. Under the driver's seat, in the corner, he finds a basket full of scarlet nerines. He picks them up, smells them, looks around then drops them back inside the cart. Someone is playing a sick game. A sick game fraught with Guernsey folklore. Do they expect he'll believe she's been taken by fairies?

A horse whinnies behind him. Hooves clomp. Marshall clasps his sword. Dread sucks away his breath. It's not there. He turns.

"Lady Delia! Thank God I found you." Dread transforms to relief. She stares at him. The stallion fights for control. She's mounted astride. Astride a black stallion? Relief changes to confusion. "What are you doing? Where have you been?"

The stallion circles, slinging his head up, down, and side-to-side wrestling for control. Something's strange about her. Her glare, determined, steady and firm. Wild and frazzled hair is now fastened to the side below her ear. "Are you going to answer?"

Nothing. Confusion becomes worry.

Lady Delia turns, kicks the stallion, and bolts down the edge of the Braye. Straight for Le Pont du Valle. What the devil is wrong with her? He jumps up into his cart and hangs his lantern on the pole behind his seat to follow her to the bridge. No way to catch up to her. At least he'll find out where she's going. And what the deuce is going on. Where did she get the clothes she was wearing?

"Mel?" Delia's mind races. Why is Mel here? The ground is cold. Delia struggles to speak. Still, words will not come. Tears sting Delia's eyes. Tree bark scratches against her back. Not the soft, fluffy blankets she envisioned earlier.

"No time for tears. We need to get you out of here before they return."

Delia grabs a tight hold on Mel's arm and doesn't move. Two years. It's been two years since their father separated them. All Delia wants is to throw her arms around Mel and never let go.

"I know, Dee. Try to stay calm. I think they drugged you. This island is full of those calling themselves spell casters. Bunch of gibberish. Probably used an herb or other plant given to us from God himself." Mel tugs Delia's arms to try to pull her to her feet. "It'll wear off soon. We need to move. Now. Whatever they did to you, they're going to regret it."

Mel. Always protective. Always to the rescue. Delia's feet slog the ground. Heavy. Mel's right. Drugged.

"We need to get you on the horse." Mel's voice is winded.

Delia nods agreement. Her body moves like a stuffed doll. She lifts her leg to the stirrup. Each move aches. No strength either. She grabs hold of the pommel and pulls. Mel shoves from behind. The horse moves his backside away. Not helping.

"Wait. Put your foot here. I'll lift you up." Delia looks down at Mel's intertwined fingers forming a step. She steps in, Mel lifts, the horse moves over. Only one thing to do. She throws her arms around Mel and hangs on. It doesn't help. She still falls. Face down and flat on top of Mel. Cart wheels roll alongside of them. It's too late. Her captors are back.

"What's this?"

Evening air chills her bum. She yanks the fabric down. Mel struggles under her. Mel's blue eyes and upturned lips threaten to erupt. Really? Now is not the time to fall into a fit of laughter.

Lord Daventry glares down at both of them. No humor there. How can she explain? If only her words would come.

"Lady Delia!" Marshall toggles from one and then the other. Astounding. No difference except the clothes they're wearing—or lack of. "How—how is it possible?"

The other Lady Delia answers. "Do you really need an explanation?" Both ladies stand up.

"Of course not. It's clear you're twins, but why here?" Still bouncing from one twin to the other, his focus lands on *the* Lady Delia. "Why now?"

The one in black answers instead. "She can't talk."

"What do you mean she can't talk?"

"I mean she's been drugged. I've seen it before."

"Before?"

"In France."

"Who are you, exactly?"

"Mel." The one called Mel wraps her arm around Lady Delia's waist.

"Fine. Mel it is for now, but I certainly will not continue to refer to you as that since you are clearly Lady Delia's sister." Lord Daventry holds them back. "Before we go anywhere, explain how she ended up here, drugged, and where you've been these last two weeks since her arrival?" Lady Delia looks at her black-clad companion.

Mel pushes past and helps her sister move forward. "Now is not the time. Let's get out of here before they come back."

"Do you know who they are?"

Mel hands Marshall her horse's reins to hold him steady while she helps Lady Delia mount. "Best not find ourselves at their mercy."

"So you do know who they are."

Mel joins her sister on the back of her horse and turns to leave. "I may know *of* them."

CHAPTER FOUR

"Delia, please. Drink it. You'll feel better." Delia's heart ricochets in her chest. Unease creeps through her pores. That's what the crotchety woman with long gray hair said.

"I can't." Delia holds her hands in front of her face, turns her head, and looks out the window. Early morning sunshine highlights green lawns seasoned with color, hedge rows, and topiaries. Sausmarez Manor. Not home, but safe. Safe from the tomb, safe from the people who took her, safe.

Mel tries holding the tea to Delia's mouth again. "Why not?"

Delia shakes her head. Its hot aroma touches the end of her nose. Distressed pangs radiate into her sides. "It was the tea. It must have been the tea."

"What was the tea?" Mel sets the cup on the circular nightstand.

"That woman gave me warm tea to drink. The next thing I remember, I'm lying on my back in the cart. Unable to talk." Mel can't possibly understand the feeling of being taken. Taken against your wishes.

"That sounds about right." Mel leans back in the floral brocade armchair.

"What do you mean?"

"When I was in France, I stayed with a woman for a time, a healer." Mel outlines the red and blue flowers on the armrest with her forefinger.

"Healing? I hardly think I was given a healing elixir."

"No."

"Wait. You were in France? When?" Delia presses her fists into each side of the bed to sit up.

"It doesn't matter." Mel leans back, props her legs up on the edge of the bed, and crosses them at the ankle.

"Of course it matters! I haven't seen you in two years. I had no idea you'd made it all the way to France."

Mel inspects the ends of her finger nails. "Try India."

"How is that possible? Does Papa know?"

Mel bites the tip of her forefinger. "Does he know? Delia—he sent me there." She sputters the remnant toward the floor.

"Oh. I'm so sorry. I had no idea."

Mel puts her feet back on the floor, resting her elbows on her knees. "You didn't wonder what happened to me?"

"Of course I did! I thought Papa was away so long looking for you."

Mel sits back again. "He was having me shipped to India." Maybe Mel does understand being taken. "Didn't you ask where I was? Where I went?"

Delia fidgets with the fabric of the blanket. "I asked Mama."

"What did she tell you?"

"She said you left. You know Mama and how she is." Delia's broken heart beats farther into two pieces. Two years. Two long years alone without Mel. She believed the worst.

"And?"

"I thought it was Mama's way of telling me you ran off again." Delia's soft words do nothing. Mel still fidgets, annoyed and unsettled.

"Really, Delia. You act like I was in the habit of running off." Mel picks at the side of her middle finger.

"But Mel, you did run off."

"It was one time, Delia. One time. Hardly a habit."

Delia closes her eyes and breathes in. How could she have thought the worst? The sister who has always been there for her. Always protected her. Always kept her safe. "Why India?"

"Why do you think? To marry me off." Delia's heart splits in two. How did Mel endure it?

"What was it like?"

"Hot." Of course. Making light of an uncomfortable situation is Mel.

"But did you meet anyone?"

"Yes—a lot of Indians." Delia rolls her eyes to the ceiling. Can she ever be serious?

"Not even one British soldier?"

"The last person I intend to marry is a British soldier." Now that's serious Mel. She'd rather die. Too many filtered through the household growing up. Too many.

"It's not like you have a line of dukes standing in wait."

"I'm not interested in dukes either." Mel stands up and pulls the blanket closer to Delia's chin.

"Mel. You ran off with the footman." Delia sinks down into the bed. "Don't tell me you're still hoping for him?"

"What? No! And I didn't run away with him." Mel tucks the edges under Delia's legs. A tight cocoon.

"Did you or did you not sneak out of the house? At night. Alone. With Mr. Cookson?"

Mel sits on the side of the bed. "I wasn't running away *with* him."

"What do you call it then?"

"Not what you're thinking. And not what Papa and everyone else believes." Mel tucks a stray curl behind Delia's ear.

"Did you try explaining it?"

"What do you think? Of course I did. He won't listen. He never listens."

"Who never listens?" Honoria Rutledge, Countess of Deloraine opens the door, walks in, and places herself on the side of the bed between her daughters.

Mel rolls her eyes and puffs out a deep breath between her teeth.

"Come, come, girls." Lady Deloraine wraps her arm around Mel and squeezes. "Who never listens?" She kisses Mel on the cheek then proceeds to clap her hands together twice for emphasis. "I'm listening. Right here, right now."

"It's nothing. Mel and I were catching up on old gossip."

Lady Deloraine clicks her tongue. "You know how I feel about gossip. We'll have none of that." She plumps the pillow around Delia's head and notices the tea sitting on the side table. "You haven't even finished your tea."

"I can't, Mama."

"Oh, come now. It will be good for you." Lady Deloraine moves the cup closer to her daughter's lips, but Delia raises her hand to cover her mouth. "Delia, you must."

"Mama, she doesn't want it. Can't you see?"

Lady Deloraine glares at both daughters, one at a time, before setting the tea back on the night stand. "Headstrong. Not one, but two headstrong daughters. Not a thought for what you've put me through." More eye rolls from Mel follow.

"Me?" Delia's voice screeches like her father's favorite mare. "How can you say a thing like that to me? I've always done what I'm told."

"Done what you're told? Who told you to sneak away with Daventry? To a tomb? I know I haven't."

"Mama! We didn't sneak away. He was giving me a tour of the island. Someone sealed us in."

"What are you talking about? Sealed you in." Lady Deloraine shakes her head. "Really, Delia. Who ever heard of such a thing. Where was your maid? Hmm?" Lady Deloraine crosses her arms across her chest.

"I hadn't intended on being out with him. I started out alone, he met me near the gate, and asked me to join him."

"It's no matter." Lady Deloraine readjusts the blanket under her daughter's chin. "Laurie will be back in a day or two. Your father will have it out with Daventry, and then at least one of my daughters will be out of the marriage mart."

"What?" Delia flings the blanket off. "You expect me to *marry* Daventry? I've only just met the man."

"That's plenty of time, dear. Your father and I only met once before the arrangements were made. Daventry's quite the catch, I'm told. You should be pleased."

"Pleased?"

"Of course."

Delia shoots a glance at Mel. Her tight lips and shaking head leave no doubt. None whatsoever to what she's thinking.

"But Mama, what about our plans to tour the continent? We were only to be on Guernsey Island for a short stay."

"Plans can change, dear." Lady Deloraine reestablishes the blankets for Delia and folds them at her waist. Satisfied, conniving lips are spread across her mother's face. "You can honeymoon the continent with your husband. I don't mind."

"I'm not going to marry Daventry!" Delia crosses her arms in front of her chest and slams both of her outstretched legs hard on top of the bed.

"Don't be silly, child." Lady Deloraine pats Delia's errant legs, stands up, kisses her on the forehead, and presses her cheeks between her hands. "I'm so glad you weren't harmed by those fortune tellers. I don't know what I would have done if they got away with you."

"Fortune tellers? How can you possibly know that?"

"Who else would they be?" Lady Deloraine turns to Mel and places the same mother's kiss on her forehead. "I'm so glad we found you. I've missed you so much. As soon as your sister is married, you and I can tour the continent together, hmm?" Mel turns her face away and doesn't answer.

Delia wages another strike at the bed. "Mama, I refuse!" Lady Deloraine ignores her outburst and turns to walk to the door. Typical. "It's humiliating. How can I even face the man? He's being forced to marry me."

Lady Deloraine rests her hand on the door knob and turns to face her daughter. "Don't over exert, dear, you'll have plenty of time to work it out. We're having a small gathering as soon as your father confirms the arrangements."

"Excuse me?" The throb in her throat cuts her breath short.

"I've already spoken with Sausmarez. He's given me permission to make the necessary preparations since his girls are visiting London. I've spoken with the housekeeper and plans have already started."

"Admiral Sausmarez has returned?" Delia chokes on her own dry-mouthed screech. Mel hands her the tea. Delia shakes her head. Still a no on that account.

Lady Deloraine claps her hands together in front of her chin. "Delia, aren't you listening? I just told you he's given me permission, haven't I?"

Delia tries to swallow. Her tongue sticks to the roof of her mouth. "Is Papa with him?"

"Your father will be back soon. He and the admiral have business to discuss." Lady Deloraine clasps her hands under her chin, prayerful concentration. "I'm so excited. I must go write the invitations. I'll return shortly to check on you." Lady Deloraine spins around, opens the door, and leaves. Her steps echo down the hall.

Tears fill Delia's eyes. She sinks back into her pillows. Mel leans forward and grabs hold of her hand. "Don't worry Dee. We'll figure something out." Mel's red-faced scowl leaves no doubt. And the repeat of two words. "Never listens."

"But Mel, how did you even know to come get me? How did you know we were on the island?"

Mel inhales a deep breath. "I didn't."

Delia covers her sister's hand with her own. "I don't understand."

Mel moves closer to Delia on the side of the bed and repositions a stray lock of Delia's hair. "It's not complicated, actually. I was in France and decided to come to the island for a spell. To decide where to go next. Maybe the Americas."

Delia sits up straighter. "You're not still considering going, are you? Not now?"

Mel stares down at their clasped hands. "Anyway, Ozanne was rounding up help at the pub and I overheard. Truth be told, I wasn't sure if it was you so I followed and watched. I saw them take you. Either way, I knew I couldn't let them abduct a young girl, regardless. I bided my time for my chance to speak with you, make sure it was really you. Long story short, I thought about getting help when I ran into Daventry, then I decided it was better to get you myself since I didn't know who I could trust. End of story."

Delia yawns. "I'm so happy you're back with us. There is no way I'm letting you leave for the Americas. Not now." Delia snuggles back down under the covers.

"We'll see. A lot has happened since last we were together."

"It doesn't matter. You're home now." Delia's eyes begin to shut. Mel's kiss to her forehead comforts her. Mel's soft, whispered words escape her as she drifts back to restful sleep.

Marshall pulls up to the entrance of Sausmarez Manor and hands the reins to the stable boy. Today's dig was long but worth it. Is two days enough time to recover from entrapment? He hops down, knocks, and is shown to the drawing room.

Lady Deloraine stands up from the cream-colored couch. "My lord?"

He ignores the question. His thoughts are filled with one thing. One person. "May I inquire as to the health of Lady Delia?"

Lady Deloraine delicately shifts a strand of hair away from her mouth, back into place. "Of course, you may. I should be quite offended if you did not inquire as to the health of your soon to be. Please have a seat."

He follows the line of her outstretched hand. He doesn't sit. Instead, he glares straight back into her eyes. Round and determined eyes. "I beg your pardon. My what?"

Marshall knows exactly what. He chooses to remain standing. Gather his composure albeit only for a few seconds. He swallows hard.

"Your soon-to-be wife, of course. Laurie, that is Lord Deloraine, will no doubt discuss the arrangements as soon as he returns to the island, I'm sure."

"Arrangements?"

Lady Deloraine's head nods yes. Marshall fights the urge to slap her stupid, satisfied, smiling face. She sits back down and swipes invisible dust off the round armrest before carefully placing her arm along it. He returns his own pseudo smile.

"Certainly, you did not expect anything less after spending an entire evening alone with my daughter in a locked dungeon?" Maybe she sealed them into the tomb? If he didn't believe it impossible, he might consider it probable.

Marshall coughs and wipes his forehead with his handkerchief. "Um, it was not a locked dungeon, my lady." She can hardly be serious. "It was a dolmen."

"That *is* what I said."

"No— "

"No?" Lady Deloraine stands up again from where she is sitting. "You ruin my daughter's reputation and then refuse to set things right?"

"No, my lady. You misunderstand. I was referring to the tomb, that is, the dolmen."

"What do you mean *tomb*?"

This is not going as expected. "The ancient burial site? The place we were sealed in?"

"What? You took my daughter to the catacombs? What sort of gentleman are you, Daventry?"

The woman can't be serious. "I can assure you—"

"Luring innocent young ladies to places where they can catch who knows what. It's no wonder she couldn't speak when she was found."

"Now, that— " Marshall raises his forefinger to point out the facts.

"Probably a mummy's curse."

Will the woman ever shut up? "Lady Deloraine. There is no such thing. Propaganda, balderdash."

Lady Deloraine raises her chin in the air, and her half-closed eyes attempt to look down on him, even while she sits. "I'm afraid I must insist. If you won't make things right, I'll have no choice but to speak to Sausmarez about the matter."

"Sausmarez? What does he have to do with it?"

"He *is* the local magistrate, if I'm not mistaken."

"Things do not operate the same in Guernsey. This is not England."

"Of course it's not England. Admiral Sausmarez is a member of Nelson's band of brothers. I've no doubt he'll hear my petition and agree. We may even have the ceremony performed aboard his ship, the *Orion*."

"The O—What?" Marshall holds his forehead with one hand and places the other on his hip. The woman is mad. If she thinks she can dictate to Sausmarez what will happen in his own home...

The door to the drawing room opens. Lady Delia. Relief, at least for a moment. The second Miss Rutledge follows.

"Mama? What's going on? We can hear you all the way down the hall. What's got you in such a tizzy?"

"Tizzy? Really child." Lady Deloraine flips open her fan. "It's only been a day and already Carmella's forming you to her ways."

"Me?" Lady Carmella flattens her hand to her chest. "I have no control over Delia."

"Mama, don't avoid the question."

Marshall takes a seat on the side. Lady Delia's floral scent whiffs by when she passes. His attention is immediately drawn to her hourglass shape, the swish of her gown, and the soft tap-tap of her walk complementing the sway of her curvy hips. He needs to think. To decide. He watches.

"Delia, if you must know. Daventry and I were discussing your upcoming nuptials."

"Daventry? Our what?" Lady Delia spins around and stares at Marshall. He shrugs. What else can he do?

She glares back at her mother. "Absolutely not. I will not. There was no harm done."

"No harm? You were locked in a dungeon for who knows how long, *alone* together, before being dug out in front of the whole town." Marshall imagines the breeze from Lady Deloraine's fan must be the cause of the cool settling around him. Whatever the source, it's refreshing. He tugs the edges of his cravat near his neck. The air is stifling.

"Mama, it wasn't a dungeon. And it wasn't the whole town." She turns back to Marshall. "Say something."

"I— " Once again, he's not able to complete a sentence before the entire conversation starts from the beginning.

Lady Deloraine raises one eyebrow. The fan slaps shut. "Who said anything about a dungeon?"

"Mama, we agreed to wait until Papa returns before moving forward with any formal announcements."

"Of course, dear. This evening's dinner party is only a small gathering." Lady Deloraine opens the closet, separates and scans one gown and then another, pulling each out for a moment before stuffing it back in. "Think of it as an opportunity to get to know each other." She pulls out an elegant emerald green, running her fingers along the lacy gold trim. "The more you get to know one another before the wedding, the easier the transition will be into married life."

"Mama! I'm not getting married." Delia wants to crawl under the bed and stay there. She'd rather spend the day with the chamber pot than be forced into the company of a man who doesn't want her.

"This will do. You're far past the age of pastels. The silk will look nice against your skin."

"Mama, please stop." Breakfast coils its way back to her mouth. Tart, bitter flavors collide with her tongue.

"Why should I stop? Your life will be changing soon. You need to become accustomed to it." Lady Deloraine pats her daughter's hand and lays the gown across the bed. "Tell Daisy, or is it Lily? I can't remember the servants' names. Anyway, tell whoever she is to have it pressed for this evening." Lady

Deloraine moves out the door and down the hall before the door closes shut.

Delia shakes her head. "She never listens."

"Dee, you should be used to it by now. It's just the way she is."

Mel's worried too. She only calls her Dee when it's serious. And this is serious.

"Em, you're not the one being forced into a marriage." It's been a long time since Delia has felt close to her twin. Dee and Em. It's what they used to call each other when they were children playing dress up. This is not a game. It's dress up for real.

Mel leans back in the same brocade chair. The same one she sat in the night Delia was rescued. Mel positioned it in front of the window, her legs propped on the sill and her ankles crossed. Mel stares at the gown spread across the bed and folds her hands behind her head. "Hmm. I'm thinking I might wear emerald green. What do you say? We could use a good diversion, yes?"

"Mel. No." Delia shakes her head. Mel's form of "fun" will have them both on the shelf. For good. "I could never."

"Sure, you can. We used to do it all the time. Dee and Em, remember?"

"Of course, I remember. But we're grown now. It's been too long. Do you even remember how to wear a dress?"

"I'm wearing one now, aren't I?"

"Yes, but you're not even sitting like a lady with your feet propped up like that. And riding boots?"

Mel clomps her boot-clad feet to the floor in unison and leans forward, resting her elbows on her knees. "Come now, Dee. We used to enjoy many such adventures."

Mel is right. They did. Who's going to notice? No one here knows them. Really knows them. Avoiding Mama will be a challenge. One that makes it all the more entertaining. "As long as I get to decide what dress of yours I'm wearing."

"Deal."

"Freddie!" Marshall gives his friend from school a firm handshake and clips him on the shoulder. A friendly face. He doesn't care if his welcome is less than acceptable on such a formal occasion. Freddie clasps Marshall's hand between his own and shakes back with the same amount of vigor. It's good to see an old friend. Lady Deloraine's "small gathering" is anything but.

Freddie steps back to allow an elderly gentleman dressed in military attire to come forward. "Marshall, may I introduce to you my cousin, Colonel Joshua Gosselin. You've heard me talk of his many achievements."

"Yes, of course." Big age difference between the two. Marshall bows a formal acknowledgment. "I've long admired your landscapes of the island, sir. You are most welcome to our dinner party."

"Thank you, my boy. Frederick has told me many stories of you also."

"I'm sure he has, but has he told you he's the reason for my success in archeology?"

"Oh?" Colonel Gosselin turns to his young cousin and raises one eyebrow. "Frederick?"

Freddie shakes his head and looks to the ceiling. "He exaggerates."

"I certainly do not. If Freddie hadn't shared with me his enthusiasm in his quests for lost treasures, I never would have pursued my own career in archeology."

"Really, Frederick. Lost treasures?" The colonel's lips rise at each corner. Humor and pride battle for dominance.

"Daventry is playing."

"I assure you, I am not jesting, and we did find treasures during our exhibitions. What do you call—"

"Yes, yes, Marshall, no need to go into the details of our exploits. I'm sure Colonel Gosselin and I are more inclined to meet your fiancée?" Freddie steps in the middle of both his cousin and Marshall, linking one arm into each of theirs and walks them farther into the room near the refreshments.

Marshall stops and stares at Freddie. "My what?" His stomach dives to his toes. He knows he heard right. Still, he needs clarification, confirmation. Colonel Gosselin takes a glass from the table and sips.

"That *is* the reason for the ball, is it not?" Freddie's words are low. Maybe no one else heard.

"I'm not exactly sure." Two words and one face pop to the front of Marshall's brain. Lady Deloraine. Now what?

Freddie leans in closer to his side. "What? Didn't you offer for her?"

"No. Maybe. It's complicated." Sink. Sink into the floor and disappear. If only.

"Riiiight." Freddie's one word, wide eyes, and blank expression are clear. He'll need to do some explaining later. "I did have a chance to discuss with the colonel the recent events regarding your fiancée's—"

"Lady Delia's."

"Right. Lady Delia's abduction and what might have caused her to become paralyzed."

"And?"

The colonel's voice interrupts their conversation. His attention is focused back on them. "Monkshood. It's the only explanation."

"I've never heard of it. Lady Delia's sister said she had seen a similar occurrence in France but wouldn't elaborate."

The colonel finishes his drink, steps between them, and lays one arm on each of their shoulders. "Let's talk."

"First..." Marshall pivots them in the direction of Lady Deloraine. "Let me introduce to you the hostess."

"Lead on."

CHAPTER FIVE

Delia bites her bottom lip and swallows hard. She sleeks each hand down the sides of Mel's velvet, sapphire dress before clasping them in front of her. Why did she let Mel talk her into this? She looks over at her sister wearing the silk, emerald dress her mother laid out earlier. No one is going to be amused by their scheme. Lord Daventry is heading straight for Lady Deloraine. Two other gentlemen are with him. She turns to her sister. "Look. What should we do? Mama will want to bring them to us to introduce them."

"Don't worry. We'll avoid it and let Daventry introduce us separate from Mama."

"I think we should stop before it's too late." What's the point?

"Dee. Relax. All you have to do is follow my lead." Delia is anything but relaxed.

"Follow your lead? That's what I've been doing and look where we are?"

"Don't you remember the excitement?" No. Delia doesn't remember. She does remember the squeamish wreck ripping her insides out. For what? So Mel can satisfy childish whims?

"Let's dance." Mel grabs her hand and drags her toward the dance floor. "I'll help you remember."

"Wait—"

"The cheer..."

"What are you doing?"

"The freedom..."

"Mel, stop." Delia jerks her hand away. "Tell me what we're doing?"

"We're going to dance, silly." Mel reaches for Delia's hand again. Sparkling, giddy, and diverting Mel won't take no for an answer.

Delia clasps both hands around Mel's one. She scuffles behind Mel to the center of the dance floor. "No one has asked us." Mortification seeps into Delia's pores. Every one of them.

"We're going to dance together."

"No. No-no-no-no."

"Why not? It's not England. It's a small gathering. No one is going to care." Delia pulls to leave. Mel pulls back. Mel wins.

A gravely throat clears behind her. "May we join you?" Delia steps back into the man who belongs to the crushed-rock voice. The marquess. Mel takes a stance beside her. Lord Daventry's dark blue tailcoat and camel color breeches enhance his muscular form in every aspect. Swarms of flutters swim in her stomach. He's handsome, dashing, delectable, and absolutely... Dark brown eyes absorb all her words, all her thoughts. Why hasn't she noticed before now?

"Well?"

His question brings her back. Mel's pinch to her upper arm helps. "Of course." How can she say no?

"First, may I introduce my closest friend from school, Freddie, er, Mr. Frederick Corbin Lukis."

"Freddie, this is Lady Cordelia Rutledge and her sister Lady Carmella Rutledge."

"Nice to meet you, Mr. Lukis."

Freddie bows to Mel first, then Delia. Now comes trouble. Lord Daventry recognizes them both. He introduced them correctly. What's Mel going to do now?

A new song begins. Mr. Lukis turns to Mel. "May I have this next dance?"

Mel doesn't even flinch. "Why not dance with my sister for this one, and I shall dance the next with you?"

What. Is. Mel. Doing?

"Of course." Mr. Lukis's sudden furrowed brow is replaced by a wide, bright smile when he turns to Delia and offers his hand. Delia widens her eyes at Mel. This is not exciting. Not fun, not freeing, not in the least.

Lord Daventry intercepts. "If you don't mind, I should like the first dance with you, myself." He steps in the middle between her and his friend, wraps his arm around Delia's waist, pulling her close to his side while guiding her onto the dance floor before anything else is said. Of course, it's a waltz. Maybe a little exciting.

"Care to tell me what's happening?"

"I'm not sure what you mean." The touch of his hand holding hers, coupled with the other one grasping the side of her waist, scrambles rational thought from her mind. The orange spice scent of him doesn't help. She can't speak much of anything. She can't even look up, instead focusing on blips of color passing by over his shoulder while they dance.

Dare she look at his face? Dare she look into his sharp, dark brown...

"My lady?"

What is the matter with her?

Lord Daventry positions his face in front of hers, forcing her to look at him. "I know it's you, Delia. May I call you Delia? What I don't understand is why you and Lady Carmella are masquerading as each other."

How did he know? No one except their parents have ever been able to figure it out. She can't form words. Almost like her reaction from the tea. Almost. Except she hasn't had any tea. Definitely not diverting. Call her Delia?

"Delia, talk to me. If you're in trouble, I can help."

His soft and kind words are what she needs to hear. Like a kiss against her cheek. What would his kiss feel like? She turns her head a smidgen to peek. Their lips, a breath away. Of course, he can call her Delia. Warmth creeps up her neck, her cheeks, all the way to the scalp of her head. Warm, kind eyes melt her. Not sharp at all. Her words, finally, are whispers. "I'm not in trouble."

Trouble is exactly what she's in. Her words tickle Marshall's lips. Her blushes and lavender fragrance spur him on. His insides are hot. Being this close to Delia was not his intention. Feeling anything for her, not his intention. He doesn't want to let her go. The trembles under his touch jar his sensibilities. He wants to take her away. So he does.

Marshall dances her off the floor, out the door, straight to the patio outside, as fast as the one, two-three, one, two-three rhythm will allow.

"I'm not sure this is a good idea." Delia's words are faint, but she keeps in step with him.

Marshall offers her a seat on a bench near the balustrade. "It's certainly not worse than being sealed inside a tomb." He sits as close as he can next to her. The side of his leg touches hers. She doesn't move. He doesn't either.

"How did you know?"

"Delia, you and your sister are not as identical as you think."

"No one has ever guessed before."

"That you know of."

"We've done it for years."

"Why?"

"I honestly can't remember. I guess young whims, excitement, a little rebellion."

"I can understand that." No question Marshall is excited. Probably not her intention. Probably not the same.

"I still can't believe you guessed."

"You are not your sister. Your eyes are different, and you have a group of freckles below them that are clearly different from your sister's." He brushes the back of his forefinger along the top of her cheek. He can't help it. Some part inside moves him like a puppet. He wants to touch her. "Even your hair is different." He twists a wisp around the same finger and lingers just for a second, before allowing the back of his hand to run along her jawline.

Silence splits the air between them. His own explanation surprises him. His reaction to her causes angst. The kind he gets whenever he's about to follow an instinct on a new discovery. The kind he gets when he sees it for the first time. The kind he gets when he touches it the first time. Delia's cheeks glow a light pink and she faces forward. Marshall coughs.

Delia inhales a deep breath. "It was Mel's idea. We used to dress up and switch places all the time when we were younger. We would become Dee and Em."

"Dee and Em?"

"Dee for Delia and Em for Mel."

"Ah. So tonight's plan was to accomplish, what exactly?" Marshall moves over slightly to put a small space between them. Very small. He focuses more on their words and less on the woman. The woman sitting close. Very close.

"Nothing, really. Mama is intent on how she wants things. Tonight was about rebellion, I guess. And, of course, she never listens."

"Oh? I hadn't noticed." That earns him a delicious smile and a toxic giggle. He enjoys her laugh. He wants to hear more, but her lips switch to a pout.

"I'm sorry." Her voice is softer now.

"For?"

"For Mama. For this ball. For everything. I will find a way to make things right."

"Hmm. And how do you propose to do that?"

"I don't know yet. But I do know I don't want to force anyone into marriage."

"Delia, I can assure you I will not be forced to do anything I don't wish to."

"Why, then, are you here?"

"Because I was invited. No one declines an invitation to Sausmarez." He doesn't want to see her sad. He reaches over to hold her hand in his. Only to comfort her. He expects her to pull away. She doesn't. A dog barks in the garden behind them. The mutt. "Apparently, he thinks he's invited too."

That scores another giggle, but then the silence returns. Delia stares at her lap and their tangled hands. "He should be invited. It's all because of him we're here."

"Maybe. There's also the matter of you being my fiancée." Where did that come from? The last thing he wants is marriage.

"Your what?" She pulls her hand away.

Emotions conflict with reason. "I only just found out myself." Marshall leans back against the balustrade and crosses his ankles in front.

"Explain?"

"I don't know exactly how, yet, but apparently the word is out."

"'The *word* is out?" Delia turns slightly toward him. "Nothing has been published. No banns have been read. Do they even read the banns in Guernsey? I don't understand. Mama promised. Promised only a small gathering to get more acquainted." She swivels to face forward again. Her rattled questions amuse him.

Marshall crosses his arms behind his head. "She clearly didn't keep her promise or she found a way around it. This is no small gathering, according to Guernsey society."

Delia stares forward after exhaling another deep breath. "I don't know what we're going to do."

He can't hold off any longer. The puppet master takes control. "The only thing we can do." He reaches in front of her, lifts her chin toward him, and touches her lips with his.

Delia's heart is racing. She touches her lips. The sensation of Lord Daventry's mouth on hers lingers, teasing her palette like an exquisite French wine. Why didn't she stop him? Warm tendrils of something continue to make her stomach swim. She makes a conscious effort to place each foot forward. Keep going. Don't look back. Tears sting the back of her eyes. He must think her a doxy. She is a doxy. Only a doxy would allow a man to kiss her that way. And enjoy it.

A hand reaches from behind a tall, potted, plant and grabs her arm as soon as she walks through the patio doors. Mel.

Mel drags her into a corner nook and sits her down. "Where have you been?"

"I-I was..."

Mel isn't listening. She peers around the corner before sitting down next to Delia. "I've been looking for you. One minute you're waltzing around the dance floor, the next, *poof!* I can't find you anywhere. Where's Daventry?"

"He's—"

"It doesn't matter." Mel stands up, leans around the corner again then sits back down, hikes her dress up above her knees, clunks the back of her head against the wall, and closes her eyes in the process.

"Mel, what's wrong?"

"Nothing."

"It's not nothing. Who are you hiding from?"

"I'm not hiding. Maybe I am a little. It's been a long time since I've had to be dressed like this. Constantly aware of my walk, my speech, everything." Mel sticks her tongue out and makes a pseudo gag. "How do you stand it?"

"I—" Delia pauses, waiting for Mel to interrupt. She doesn't. Instead, she's waiting. Waiting for Delia to answer. "I don't know. I just do."

Of all the nights for Mel to acknowledge her. Of all the nights for Mel to seek her out for help. Of all the nights. It has to be this night. The night marking the first time she's ever done anything remotely close to scandalous. Lord Daventry's kisses still burn hot in her memory. Warmth rises in her cheeks.

"Delia, what's wrong?" She turns away from Mel to hide it. If Mel finds out, who knows how she'll react. Anything from defending a sister's honor to wanting details of the event. One extreme to the other.

"Nothing."

Mel leans forward to try to see her face. "Look at me." Delia turns her face to avoid her, stands up, and moves back into the ballroom. "Delia, wait."

Mel catches up to her by the refreshment table. Colonel Gosselin and Mr. Lukis are there sipping punch. Not exactly where she wants to be at this moment. Lord Daventry will be at her side sooner than she would like if she remains in their company.

"Daventry!" Too late. "Where have you been hiding?" Mr. Lukis steps to the side to allow him to join their circle. The marquess moves to Delia's side, allowing his arm to brush hers. A flush of new warmth waves through her senses. Again. She ignores Mel's incoherent whispers. One thing is clear. Mel knows.

"Just outside for a change of scenery."

"Ah, yes. Lovely evening it is." Mr. Lukis sips his punch in one long slurp then places his empty glass on the table next to them. "The colonel and I were continuing our discussion of the monkshood with, er..." Mr. Lukis furrows his brow and looks at one sister and then the other. "Lady...Rutledge."

Lord Daventry grabs a glass of champagne from a servant's tray passing by. "And?"

Colonel Gosselin also reaches for a glass from the tray, and then takes a second one to offer to Mel. Of course she drinks more than a sip and places the empty glass back on the tray. The colonel then grabs a third glass for Delia. "Here, child. You look pale. This might help put some color in your cheeks."

Mel intercepts the glass. "I think she's had enough color for this evening." Another Mel-gulp follows.

Delia glares at her sister and purses her lips. Will she understand her meaning? Too much champagne never turns out well.

"What? I haven't had champagne in ages." Mel sips this time and winks at Delia. Apparently not.

Delia remains silent. What happened on the patio rewinds and plays over and over in her mind.

"One can never have enough champagne." Mel places her second empty glass on the table.

Delia peeks over at Lord Daventry. No reaction to her sister's comments. His focus is on Colonel Gosselin. "Continue Colonel."

Lord Daventry slides one step closer to Delia, their arms touch, elbow to shoulder, causing an outbreak of gooseflesh the length of her side. She doesn't move away. She likes being close to him, even the scent of him.

Daventry locks his hand with hers, and her insides shoot arrows in all directions. She peeks up at him again. Face forward, no reaction. None. What if someone sees? As if such contact is perfectly normal. "Tell us what you've discussed."

Delia folds their hands in the fabric of her dress. Maybe no one will notice. No use. He takes her hand and links her arm with his.

The colonel clears his throat. "My guess, and this is only a guess, of course, is that it must be monkshood. Very potent plant found in Europe."

"Tell them your theory, cousin, since monkshood by itself could prove fatal."

"Ah, yes. Thank you, Frederick. I believe it entirely possible it could be in the honey."

"I'm sorry? I thought we were talking about a flower." Delia watches Lord Daventry's lips while he asks the question. How can he stay so focused? The sensations pummeling through her body with only the touch of his hand to hers boggles her senses.

"Yes, yes. Let me explain. There are species of bees that feed from the pollen of the monkshood. It has been theorized that the bees filter the toxins when they make their honey. But, if humans consume the honey made from these bees, it could result in an event such as you experienced"—Colonel Gosselin looks at Mel and then focuses on Delia—"Lady, um, De—"

An eruption of clattering, followed by gasps mixed with barking, echoes through the halls, getting louder by the second.

Delia looks at Lord Daventry, who's holding his glass almost to his mouth to take a sip. He closes his eyes. "No. Please, no."

"What is it?"

Lord Daventry's jaw tightens. He puts his glass down and positions her behind him. Not again. Memories of the last time he positioned her in this exact same way sparks another episode of uncontrollable laughter only wet dog kisses can explain.

A mass of black, matted fur, pawing and barking his way down the corridor, across the ballroom floor, clearing an open path straight into Daventry's halting, outstretched arms. Everyone watches. Not many speak. The mutt rises on his hind legs the moment he reaches Lord Daventry and places his front paws on his shoulders. Then it begins. Wet, happy kisses. Dog kisses. Delia can't control the hilarity of it. She's not alone. The marquess can barely speak. "Good dog. Slow and steady. Let's go." Lord Daventry does the only thing he can to do. He waltzes the mutt right out the patio doors, slobbery kisses and all.

Delia starts to follow them out. Mel holds her back. "You and I need to have a conversation."

"Not now, Mel. Please."

"Girls, girls. Oh, my girls. Did you see it?" Lady Deloraine's voice cries out above the crowd while she swishes and claps her way in their direction. "Did you see the swine?"

Mel rolls her eyes to the ceiling. "Really Mama? Don't you mean dog?"

"Of course it was a dog. What else would it be?" Lady Deloraine disappears back into the crowd of her guests, calming the scene, encouraging the orchestra to play once more.

Mr. Lukis steps in to assist the situation. "Maybe now might be a good time for a dance, Lady Delia?"

Delia glares at Mel.

Mel nods once. "Go on. I don't know how, but they've guessed our little secret."

Delia turns back to Mr. Lukis and swiftly takes the hand he offers.

CHAPTER SIX

Marshall guides the mutt to the stairs leading to the lawn. One last slosh slides across his face before the mutt pushes off his chest and runs down the steps, barking his way along the lawn before disappearing around the corner of the house. Marshall wipes the side of his face with his sleeve and returns to the ballroom. A scream echoes through the air the moment he opens the patio doors. Frantic people rush in all directions.

Marshall hears one voice above the others. "He took her. That ruffian just took her." He follows it.

Marshall scans the room. Colonel Gosselin wipes blood from the corner of his lips. Freddie and several others are being helped up from the floor. Lady Deloraine lay sprawled across the chaise lounge, fanning herself with one hand and holding a bouquet of scarlet nerines in the other. What in God's green earth happened here? As soon as Lady Deloraine sees him, she sits up. "You must do something. They took her. Rose. Or Daisy? Aagh. Why are they all named after flowers?"

"Lady Deloraine." Marshall sits next to her on the edge. "Who?"

"The servant girl."

"The servant girl took Delia?" His nerves begin to whirl tighter than mummified remains.

Lady Deloraine shakes the nerines. "No! No! No! The servant girl said they left these after they took her."

"Who took who?" Marshall already knows the answer.

"Those sailor men. A whole band of them. Just marched in and took her."

"Sailor men?"

"They took Delia!" Lady Deloraine is in hysterics. "Aren't you listening?"

"And no one stopped them?"

"How could they? Lily said there was an entire band of them."

Marshall swivels around to find Freddie. Swollen and red raccoon eyes meet his. "We tried." He dabs a cold cloth over one eye and then the other. "Gads! They were fast. Too fast for us to stop, my friend."

Lady Deloraine clutches onto his arm. "Never mind that now." A servant hands her a glass of amber liquid. "You have to find her."

"I will."

Lady Deloraine downs the liquid complete. "The responsibility does fall on you, of course."

"Of course."

Kicking isn't working. Pounding isn't working. Wiggling isn't working.

"What are you doing?" Delia's upside down shrills are muffled against the backside of her captor's waist. His shoulder jabs her midsection with each step he takes. He doesn't answer, he doesn't speak. What does he want? God only knows.

He parades her out of Sausmarez Manor surrounded by his band of rogues. He sets her down only to lift her up again onto the back of a black horse, facing the opposite direction. He settles himself in the saddle, forcing her to face his chest. Delia watches his thugs mount their horses around them and then position themselves on each side.

NoNoNoNoNo. Delia shakes her head. Not again. Familiar panic builds into a flurry of flails and frantic banter. Delia fights to jump off, but he holds her tight, demanding her to stop struggling. He pulls her hands hard together and ties them with a leather band, not saying a word. She's so close she can see the color of his eyes. Strange eyes. One is brown and one is green.

"What do you want with me?"

Still nothing.

"You're not going to get away with this. Everyone saw you."

His arms tighten around her waist, pulling her close against his chest. One second later, the horse jolts forward while two more pull ahead to lead the way. They all gallop at the same pace. Almost in sync. Delia's eyes sting from the veil of dust whipped up around her.

Pray. All she can do is pray. Pray Lord Daventry can find her. Pray he can get help. Pray he's in time.

Marshall runs outside yelling instructions. Yelling for Ozanne. Yelling to ready his horse. Time keeps its distance amid the chaos. One minute to organize is too long. He mounts Aladdin, and Ozanne points to the road leading to St. Peter's Port.

"That way."

Marshall kicks. "*Yaaahh*!"

Ozanne's last words fade in the distance behind him. "Her sister is only minutes ahead of you."

Her sister. Lady Carmella. What is she on about? Now he has two damsels to rescue. Minutes pass for hours. His focus—reach the port. Hope, no pray, that's where they're headed. His prayers are answered. He watches Delia's sister reach the pier and dismount while her horse is still running. Her gown is hiked above the knee, showing boots instead of slippers. And the blade fastened around her thigh. Marshall descends just as fast. He reaches the edge and pushes past her, charging up the ramp of the *HMS Wolfe* in time to see Delia bound and gagged, standing a short distance from the Russian overlord, who's blasting orders to ready the ship for sail. The same overlord who helped free them from the dolmen.

Lady Carmella is fierce on his heels. She doesn't falter once. She pushes past. He needs to contain her before something awful happens. The overlord turns. The awful something happens before he can reach, speak, or stop her. One slap-worthy blow across the wretched man's jaw with one hand ends with Lady Carmella's knife pointed directly under his chin by the other. Marshall pauses in front of them. Praise and censure war inside. The first because he couldn't have done better himself. The latter for putting them all in danger without thought or diplomacy.

"Unbind my sister. Now." Lady Carmella's voice is hard and low. Low and serious like a dog growl with words.

Chain link snaps of click, click, click, click, click ensue. Pistols point at them from every direction. Barrages of adrenaline begin their onslaught. Lady Carmella doesn't flinch. She jabs the point of her knife deeper to prick the skin under the jawbone of her target. "Tell them. Tell them to put down their guns and unbind my sister. Now."

A toothy grin spreads across the overlord's face. "I'm afraid that can't happen."

Lady Carmella's voice rumbles firm. "It will. Or you'll be the one bound in bandages. From head to toe. I said let her go."

Delia whimpers. Marshall watches tears trickle into pools on cheekbones pushed high because of the cloth tied tight between her lips. Her hair hangs wild around her face, and the sapphire dress is ripped on the shoulder. Anger flairs inside him. His hands form balls at his side. Forget diplomacy. Lady Carmella has the right of it. He's got a plan.

Marshall steps forward. This situation must end. And fast. If he can just get close enough. "I'm sure we can work something out." He takes another step forward. "Whatever you want, I'll pay."

Lady Carmella snaps her head in his direction. "What? We're not paying him. Delia will be released. No more, no less."

The Russian overlord looks at Delia and then at her sister. "Delia?"

Loud stomps clomp up the ramp. More commands follow. A different voice bellows. "Captain Mundo! What the devil are you doing?"

Both ladies' eyes widen. Lady Carmella speaks first. "Papa?"

Henry Scott Rutledge, Earl of Deloraine, pushes past Marshall and steps between the captain and Lady Carmella, forcing her to release her grip on the knife. Lord Deloraine takes it from her while his glare remains steady on the captain. "I paid you to find my daughter, Carmella. And to bring her home to England. What the deuce are you doing snatching Delia?"

Captain Mundo switches his dumbfounded gaze between the two ladies. He opens his mouth to respond, but Lady Carmella steals his words. She snaps her attention to her father. "You paid him?"

Marshall reviews the circle of people, and a familiar sense of confusion forces the same question. "Lord Deloraine. I don't understand. This man is in your employ?"

The only response to Marshall's question is received by Captain Mundo alone, in the form of one female-infused wallop to his left jaw that puts him almost flat.

Captain Mundo straightens and grabs Lady Carmella under the arm, pulling her tight against him, nose to nose. "If your father wasn't standing right here, I'd take you over my knee myself."

Lady Carmella plants herself firm in his face and doesn't move except to jerk her arm from his grasp. "Try it." She raises her other hand only to be caught mid-swing before a second blow hits her target.

Captain Mundo shoves her back. He wipes his lip with the back of his hand. "I can assure you, that will not happen a second time."

One deep belly laugh booms through the tension between them, and all eyes switch to Lord Deloraine. He pulls Lady Carmella back. "Doesn't work." He steps between them. "If all it took was a swift kick to the backside, I wouldn't be paying England's finest privateer to find my daughter."

Delia can't believe what she's hearing. Can't believe what's happening in front of her. Tears in her eyes gloss the vision before her. Everything moves slow. A blurred image of a man walks toward her. Lord Daventry. He gently takes her hands into his and begins to untie the leather band binding her wrists. Her head and body fall against his chest. His orange spice scent teases as soon as he loosens the gag pinching the sides of her mouth. Delia clutches the cloth of his lapel in each hand. Tears break through. Daventry wraps his arms around her shoulders and holds her tight while uncontrollable sobs are muffled against him.

"Lord Daventry..."

"*Shh. Shh.* It's over."

"I thought... I thought..."

"I know. It's all right. You're safe. And you must call me Marshall."

Delia pulls back and looks up at Lord Daventry. Marshall. His dark eyes are focused only on her. "Why is this happening to me? Twice. I mean, my own father?"

Daventry brushes her cheekbone with his thumb to wipe away her tears. The soft palm of his hand and fingers linger against her cheek. "I'm sure your father would never allow harm to come to you. It was your sister they were after."

"*Pfft.* Mel. They never would have gotten this far with Mel. I mean, look."

Delia nods toward Mel, still trying to get at Captain Mundo, her father still holding her back at the waist.

"Dee. I mean Delia."

She likes the way it sounds when he calls her Dee. "You can call me Dee."

"Good. Dee. Come, let's get you back to Sausmarez."

Marshall maneuvers her around to walk her off the ship. He keeps his arm around her waist and doesn't let go of her hand. He puts himself between her and Captain Mundo as they push past.

Lord Deloraine stops them and takes control of Delia's exit. "There, there, my dear girl."

Delia looks at her father. The soft change in his voice reminds her of when she was a child running to him for protection from anything chasing her. It comforts her. Even through the chaos. Even through the mix up. He's her father. Tears build again. "Papa. I just want to go home."

"Yes, yes. Home." He pats her hand and begins to escort her down the ramp.

Mel shoves Captain Mundo and joins them. Marshall relinquishes his hold to Mel. "Excuse me, one moment."

Delia stops to watch Marshall walk back to where Captain Mundo is standing massaging the side of his face. He picks up the captain's tricorn hat and hands it to him. He places it back on his head in time for one male-infused blow to slam into its target. One man falls flat. Captain Mundo's men surround them again. Captain Mundo raises his hand while standing up. "No. Let them be."

Marshall separates the wall of sailors and follows Delia, Mel, and Lord Deloraine down the ramp and off the ship. Marshall's one-word response whispered from behind brings a smile back to her swollen lips.

"Idiot."

"Another ball? No, I'm not doing it again." Delia stands up from the table to fill her plate a second time at the sideboard. Two days. Not even two days and her mother is already starting her tirades. It needs to stop. And breakfasts at Sausmarez always require seconds. Guernsey is not England after all. No one here will comment on her two plates of food.

"Delia, dear. We cannot leave things the way they stand now. You must know this." Lady Deloraine claps her hands together twice. "Don't you see? We need to leave with a celebration, not a mockery." Lady Deloraine sips her tea but stops midway. "Take care not to eat too much. We can't have you putting on weight before your wedding."

"What?"

"They'll be plenty of time after you're married to put on weight."

"Mama! Please."

"Of course you'll gain some weight. It's to be expected, you know."

Delia rolls her eyes and piles more potatoes. And eggs. And toast. Her mouth waters, hunger gurgles in her stomach. "What do you mean by mockery? How can you think what I experienced as a mockery?"

"Not you, dear. The waif who tore through here clawing at everyone."

"The waif?"

"Oh no, no, no. Too many potatoes. Put some back. You must."

"I will not put some back and there was no waif. You mean the dog." Delia can barely contain her giggles.

"Of course it was a dog. If it wasn't for Daventry putting himself in harm's way, and for your own protection, I might add."

"Excuse me? For my protection?" Delia shoves two spoonfuls of potatoes into her mouth back to back. This entire conversation is ludicrous. Where is Mel?

Asked and answered. Late as usual. Mel sidles into the dining room, circling a path to the sideboard like a cat scoping out its prey. She stops behind Delia's chair, bending to speak next to her ear. "I doubt Delia has anything to worry about now. Daventry won't let her out of his sight. He's practically moved in from Havilland's."

Delia's spoon clanks on the plate where she drops it. "What is wrong with the two of you?" She stares Mel down all the way to where she stops to fill her plate. Intimidation doesn't work.

Mel takes a seat across from her, smiles, and stuffs a fresh baked croissant as far in her mouth as it goes before biting down. "Daventry is all about Delia's protection now. You should have seen him, Mama."

"Really?" Lady Deloraine clasps her hands in front of her mouth, ready for any pieces of juicy gossip Mel is willing to give.

Delia shakes her head. A good slap is what Mel needs. The deed is almost done before Marshall walks in with Lord Deloraine. "Join us for breakfast, Daventry." Lady Deloraine's head pivots back and forth between the two men, who each take a seat next to their respective ladies after filling their plates first. Her head stops and rests at Lord Deloraine. Waiting. "Well?"

Lord Deloraine smiles and places a napkin across his lap. "Well what, my dear?"

"Laurie, dear. What do you think? Are we making it official?"

Delia chokes on the egg in her mouth. "Official?" She snaps a glance at Marshall, who's not looking up from his plate.

Lord Deloraine turns to his lady, still smiling, and rests his head against his hand. "Darling, from what I gather, my meeting with Daventry was just a formality, hmm?" Her father surveys all the members of his family sitting around the table and stops at Marshall. "Is that all you're eating Daventry?"

"Yes, sir. I breakfasted earlier this morning with Havilland."

Marshall won't look up. Won't make eye contact. Won't make a move in her direction. It can mean only one thing. Force. Delia will not have it. She will not marry a man forced into marriage to her. Ever.

Marshall refuses to look up at her. Not after the ripping he endured from Delia's father moments ago. Lord Deloraine, or Laurie as he's known by close friends, is not to be trifled with. His expectations of their arrangement—their engagement rather—leaves no misunderstanding. Lord Deloraine observed every moment that passed between himself and Delia on Captain Mundo's ship. Any opportunity to avoid this marriage is not possible. Not now. Delia is clearly not pleased. Hell, he's not pleased. He should have kept his urges under control. Too many people observed their dalliance at the ball. Any notion of the mutt escapade overpowering the gossips is out the window. News of his rescue of Delia is only spurring them on. Delia's long, hard glare burns hot. Best not to engage. There will be plenty of time for that after she learns her father's plans for them.

CHAPTER SEVEN

"How long are you going to keep this up?" Delia continues to ignore her sister's pleas to speak to her. Until the hurt goes away or until she's satisfied Mel has suffered enough, not before.

"Dee. There is nothing you or I could have done to change it. Papa's word is final. You know how he is."

Papa's word *is* final. Too final. Delia turns around, forcing her sister to face her back. She picks up the brush from the dresser and begins brushing. Slow and steady. She watches the reflection of her face in the mirror as her natural waves straighten with each tug of the brush. Mel stands behind her and reaches to remove the brush from her hand. "Let me, Dee." Delia keeps brushing. "Please?"

Mel doesn't wait for her to relinquish the brush. Long and gentle strokes relax the nerves threatening to break. Delia watches her face and its blank expression in the mirror. It begins to blur. Mel stops brushing and kneels in front of her. She lifts Delia's chin so she can see her face. "Hey, now. Everything will turn out as it should."

"No, it will not." Tears flow down her cheek. Numb waves ooze through to her core.

Mel pulls a footstool from the corner so she can sit beside Delia. She takes Delia's hands in hers, making Delia turn to face her. "Dee, you'll be fine. Trust me."

"How can you know this?"

"Dee, honey. You know what's expected of us. We must marry. It's the way of things." Mel wipes her cheek with the back of her forefinger.

Delia sniffs. "It sounds funny hearing this from you."

"Let's just say I've come to understand some things. And one thing I know. Daventry is a gentleman. He will treat you as the lady you are. By the way he came to your rescue, I've no doubt."

"You can't know that."

"You may be surprised at what I've come to know."

"What do you mean?"

"That, my dear, is a story for another day. Not today."

What. Has. Happened to Mel? Never in their twenty-four years has her sister been like this. Wise. Almost wise beyond her years.

"Em, what is it?"

"What is what?"

"You're different."

"No. You are. You've fallen for him. Admit it. You have feelings for him. I know you do."

"I don't." Delia sniffs again. How could she have feelings for him? They've only known each other for a few short weeks. It doesn't matter if the intimacy of their kiss sends her insides loopy. It doesn't matter if the thought of being securely wrapped in his arms is the only item that erases her father's entire miserable scheme to get Mel back.

Mel hands her a handkerchief from the dresser. "Here." Delia wipes her eyes. "Clearly."

"What's that supposed to mean?"

"Only that I know my sister. If you truly didn't care for him, you wouldn't be sitting here crying about it. You'd be finding ways to call it off. And he's not awful."

That is not what Delia needs to hear. Tears flow again. Loud and free. "Mel, what am I going to do?"

Mel wraps her arms tightly around Delia, drawing her close. "You're going to dress in that lovely pink gown Mama has selected for you and make your appearance as the future Marchioness of Daventry."

Delia follows Mel's line of sight to the pink taffeta concoction strewn across her bed. "Um...hmm."

How will Delia be today? Marshall has stayed away since the meeting with her father. This evening will be different. He'll be expected to keep to her side. The official announcement will be sometime before supper. He looks at his timepiece. Where is she? Delia should have made her appearance before now. He surveys the room and greets a few guests as they trickle into the Baronial Hall. Freddie and Colonel Gosselin are among the first to arrive.

"Ready for another go?" Freddie's familiar smack across the back of his neck surprises him. Marshall offers his response in the form of a jab to the gut. Freddie jumps back in time for it to miss. "Easy there, friend."

"Sorry, you startled me."

"Not to worry. What's got you riled?" Marshall wouldn't call it riled. Lily-livered? Maybe.

"It's nothing."

"Come, now. I can see it in your face. Not ready for another dance with the rogue?"

"Excuse me? The rogue?"

"The rogue mutt, don't you know."

"Oh, him." Rogue is a good name for the scamp. "No. I've no cause for concern on that account. We have... What can I call it? An understanding?"

"An understanding?" Freddie's laugh directs all attention on them. Freddie looks around the room, lowers his head to Marshall's ear, and speaks more softly. "You speak of him like he's a person."

"What? Are you daft? A person." Marshall scoffs, but notices Freddie's smile sag. Freddie loves animals. "Hmm. Now that you mention it, I have noticed a certain level of intelligence I can't put a reason to."

Freddie's natural ease returns and his eyes light up the minute he turns toward the stairs. Shuffles and scuffles cease. Marshall follows the line of sight. Silence fills the room.

Delia pauses on the first landing during her descent from the upper rooms. Lady Carmella joins her, but Marshall's only focus is Delia. Why was she crying? Red laces the edges of her eyes. She surveys the room from above. Guilt settles in his chest. Does it have anything to do with him? Her eyes find their mark. Him. It takes all the strength Marshall has not to run up the stairs, take her in his arms, and head straight for the back rooms. Wisps of apricot hair frame her face. One thick lock hangs to the side. Her dark burgundy dress fits her sleek form, hugging all her curves. He watches her begin to descend again, caressing the dark wooden rail of the staircase on each step down. He can't help wishing he might receive the same attention. He can't help wonder. Wonder if she will ever forgive him. Wonder if he can be a husband she deserves.

Fear supplants all expression on Delia's face and freezes all his thoughts. He turns around to see what's disturbed her. A gentleman dressed in the sharpest fashion on the island makes his appearance in the entrance hall. This man hands his hat to the butler and smiles, then turns to face Delia, who's now made her way to the second landing on the staircase. Confusion turns to recognition then turns to anger, the minute he makes eye contact. Action comes next. Not by Marshall. Lady Carmella's swift decent past Delia on the stairs and an equal shot of forward momentum reaches an abrupt halt the moment she stops and raises her hand to the new arrival.

Fwap! Her wrist is caught mid-air. Again. "My lady, one might think you don't want me here." She wrestles her wrist from his grasp. The cad is laughing in the process. He enjoys it.

Lady Carmella doesn't blink. "There is no might. One doesn't want you here. No question of might. How dare you show up uninvited."

Lord Deloraine separates the small group surrounding them. "My dear. What are you doing? Let the man alone. He is invited."

Lady Carmella whirls around. "By who?"

"I invited him. Now if you will kindly step aside and allow the gentleman to pass."

"Gentleman? Hardly."

Marshall watches Lord Deloraine escort Captain Mundo through the entrance hall and into the dining room. Marshall returns his attention to the landing, but Delia is no longer there. He canvasses the area to find her snug against a wall in the corner. He exhales a deep breath. How will she react? He walks up to her and reaches out to take one of her hands in his. "How are you faring?" She doesn't shirk.

"We're speaking now, are we?"

He deserves that.

"Delia. I'm sorry. I've been trying to find the words to ask for your forgiveness."

"My forgiveness?"

"If it wasn't for me, my actions. That is, we would not be in the position we're in."

"And what position exactly are you referring to?"

She's not making it easy. "Delia, I think I know you well enough now. You would rather be anything but forced. You've said as much in the dolmen." She doesn't acknowledge his attempt to smooth things over. He decides to leave it. More pressing is how she's dealing with Captain Mundo in attendance. "Do you think you'll be able to dine in the same room with him?"

That got her attention. "Who, Captain Mundo? I think he's the one that needs to be worried with Mel in the room."

Marshall can't help but chuckle. "I can't say I disagree." No doubt Lady Carmella will find her way to deliver the blow that keeps getting stalled. "Shall we make our way to dinner then?" He offers his arm and she takes it.

"It's not entirely your fault, you know." Delia's tone is soft.

"What's that?"

"Our engagement." Marshall centers his attention on Delia. Her copper hair. Her face. Her lips twitch at the corner. Luscious, captivating, succulent lips. Lips he can't stop thinking about. And eyes, that at the moment, refuse to meet his.

"Hmm." Odd satisfaction replaces the heavy weight in his chest.

Delia sits at her assigned position next to Marshall. She watches her father at one end of the long, dinner table and Admiral Sausmarez at the other. Crystal vases with multi-colored freesia lines the middle. The admiral raises his glass for a toast while each guest is served. Mel is ready to spit fire. Captain Mundo is seated across from her, enjoying every minute of her irritation. If he only knew his cocky grin fuels that fire. Maybe he does.

Marshall's whispers tickle Delia's ear. She can't make out what he's saying. She turns her face toward him. His expression is kind. "What do you think?"

"About what?"

He leans closer to her. "Will Mel reach her target eventually?"

"Her target?"

"Captain Mundo."

"She won't stop trying. He needs to stop goading her, but I hope he doesn't. The man deserves what he'll get."

"Don't worry. I won't let him near you." Mel was right. Marshall is her protector. Delia looks across at Mel, focused and combustible. Focused on the man across the table from her and combustible enough for her father to glare the same fierceness at Mel. Delia can't help the satisfaction. She leans closer to Marshall. As close as she can without appearing too impertinent. When the explosion happens, she wants to see it.

Her father raises his glass and clears his throat. Here it comes. "I see no reason to wait any longer. Admiral, if I may?" The Admiral nods his agreement. Delia stares at her lap, fingers twisting and fidgeting with the fabric of her dress. It's not supposed to be announced until supper. Not that it matters when. She wanted to enjoy Marshall's attention a bit longer. Will he freeze up around her again? Lord Deloraine clears his throat once more while everyone silences and turns their attention to his direction. "It's my great pleasure to announce the engagement between Marshall Compton, the Marquess of Daventry and my daughter, Lady Cordelia Rutledge."

The guests sip their drinks and clap their hands. Marshall smiles and acknowledges the well wishes. Delia, still unsure of Marshall's sincerity, sips her wine and stares at the food on her plate. It's officially done. No turning back. Their easy conversation, lost.

Marshall watches Delia from a distance while she accepts the congratulations from each of the guests. The wet glow in her eyes is not from joy, he is certain. She didn't look up once from her plate after the announcement. He should be at her side. He can't. There's no denying his attraction to her. Lord Deloraine's words last evening are still fresh in his mind. "Your conduct with my daughter is reprehensible. You will marry her. You will take her back to Scotland to the family home. There you will stay. Hopefully, until the gossips are subdued with time. Do you understand?" Lord Deloraine's words ring constant in his ears. Marshall understands every word. The idea of marriage has never set well with him. Gone are his planned excavations. Gone, the trip to India. Gone. Gone. Gone. He turns to walk out onto the patio. A walk in the gardens may help clear his head. Get him back where he needs to be for Delia. Where he needs to be for this new life that awaits him. Whether he wants it or not.

One step off the veranda and warm, velvet dog tongue slathers against his hand. Marshall looks down at the rogue mutt. "It's all your fault. It can't possibly be mine."

The mutt barks and nudges his nose under the palm of Marshall's hand. "So you want to play nice today, huh?" Marshall kneels to give him a good scrub on each side of his face and below his ears. He notices for the first time the different color eyes. Right eye brown and left eye green. "Hmm. We need to come up with a name for you I think. What do you think about Rogue?" The mutt smacks his jowls and circles in place. Marshall stands back up and continues his trek through the garden. "Talk more later?"

The mutt runs ahead and barks. What is the animal chasing now? Marshall steps up his pace to close the gap in time to see the familiar red wheels of a blue cart turn the corner, leaving the grounds. The same gold-knotted symbol tinted with blue and green colors on the back catches his eye. What are they doing here? His stomach is immediately sick. No way to reach the cart now. He turns around and runs back to the manor house. He needs to find Delia. To know she is safe.

He walks into the house and scans the room. Searching. Conversations overlap. No sign of Delia. No sign of Lady Carmella. No sign of Deloraine. Marshall's head pulses and his heart pounds in his chest. Lady Deloraine is busy talking to Admiral Sausmarez, but no Delia. His fears heighten. He doesn't see her sister either.

"You look a fright." The sound of this particular voice makes him cringe even more.

Marshall turns around to watch Captain Mundo gulp half of his glass of champagne. "You're one to talk."

"True. Speech is a useless waste of time. Actions. Actions provide results."

Marshall fists his hands at his sides and takes a deep breath, still scanning the room. He'd like to take action right now. In the form of a knock-out punch to the jaw. One wasn't enough.

Admiral Sausmarez halts any further thought on that subject because he leaves Lady Deloraine and is moving straight for them.

"Captain Mundo!" Not what Marshall expects. "I heard about your most recent conquest. Outstanding!" The admiral slaps Captain Mundo across the shoulders and then reaches out to congratulate Marshall on his engagement.

"Thank you, sir." Marshall doesn't have time for this. He needs to locate Delia and make sure she's safe.

"Captain Mundo is one of England's premier privateers."

"Privateer, eh?" Pirate more like. Or bandit. Or thief. The admiral's zealous appreciation of the Captain is too much to endure. Any number of more appropriate descriptions pass through Marshall's thoughts only to be stalled at the tip of his tongue.

Captain Mundo's only response? A grunt. Where is Delia?

"Got us the best French champagne, among other delicacies of the continent." And the praise continues.

Another guttural sound from the Captain's fast-emptying glass.

Marshall continues his assessment of the party in between acknowledgments, but he still can't find Delia among the guests. He wants to punch something. Or someone. Instead he decides to stop the conversation and ask, "Have either of you seen Delia? Or Lady Carmella?"

The admiral purses his lips and surveys the room. "No. I can't say that I have."

Captain Mundo swallows the liquid currently in his mouth and mumbles. "Outside."

"What?"

"Lord Deloraine escorted both girls outside for a walk in the garden not long before you came in."

Marshall glares at England's premier privateer. "And you couldn't bring yourself to mention this to me?"

"They're with their father. You didn't ask *where* they went. Only if I had *seen* them."

"Right." Marshall takes a deep breath to avoid clobbering him. "If you'll both excuse me, I need to find my fiancée." He doesn't wait for a response. Guttural or otherwise.

CHAPTER EIGHT

Delia's heart aches, bruised and brittle. He doesn't want her. Mel may think Marshall's a gentleman, but a gentleman would not have left her side after an announcement of their engagement. Every candle in the ballroom glows golden. Pillars of flowers decorate each corner. Guests gather for dancing. The orchestra readies their instruments. Delia wants to find joy in this occasion. It's not there.

"Come with me, girls." Lord Deloraine links both daughters' arms with his and escorts them out the doors and into the garden. "A soothing walk along the floral pathways will set you to rights."

"Papa, I don't need a walk in the garden."

"I'm not asking. I'll not have you sulking. It only adds to the gabblehawkers."

Delia shoots a look at Mel, but she's not looking in her direction. "Papa, it can't look good for us to leave my own engagement party."

It's no use. He's not responding. Out the doors, down the stairs, and into garden they go. "Can we at least slow down now that we are out of the house?"

"Of course, my dear. Whatever you want." Clearly not whatever she wants, or she would not be out here at all.

A blue cart with large red-wheels pulls across the walkway ahead. Maybe it's the gardener. Mel lets go of her father's arm and reaches behind him to pull Delia back. "What is it, Mel?"

"Stop. Don't go any farther."

Her father spins around and toggles his what-the-deuce-is-going-on glare between the two of them. "Will you be sharing with us what it is?"

"It's the cart. It looks like the one they took Delia in after they pulled her out of the dolmen."

"Pulled her out of the what?"

Mel's eyes widen. She shoots Delia her silent question. Lord Deloraine stops on Delia. "Delia? Explain. What is your sister referring to?"

"Papa, I thought you knew. Lord Daventry was giving me a tour of his archaeological site at Dehus Dolman, and someone sealed us in it. "

"What the devil were you doing inside a tomb? What was Daventry thinking?"

"You didn't know? Didn't Mama tell you?"

"Your mama told me they found you in a dungeon or a cave. What's this about a tomb?"

The young servant girl, Lily, walking down the path in their direction, interrupts the conversation, a bouquet of multi-colored nerines in her hand. The cart pulls away. The gold symbol painted on the trunk reminds Delia of something. But what? She can't quite place it.

Lily pulls out an orange flower from the bouquet and hands it to Mel. She offers a white one to Delia. It's sweet floral scent lifts her mood a little. "From my father's garden. The season for them is nearing the end, and he knows how much I enjoy them so he cut me a bunch." Delia watches Lily position the brightest, pinkest flower she's ever seen in her golden hair, just behind her ear. "Wear it like this if you'd like." Lily turns her face to exhibit her profile.

She takes Mel's flower. "If I may?" She places it the same way behind Mel's ear. Mel is sharply focused on each movement Lily makes. When Lily tries to take Delia's and do the same, Mel steps between them. "I think we've got it."

"Right. Please forgive me." Lily looks to the ground, curtsies, and hurries in the direction of the house.

She crosses paths with Marshall on her way. He's almost running. He's out of breath when he reaches them. "Where did you get these?"

Delia nods toward the house. "Lily gave them to us just now."

"Never mind the flowers, Daventry. You and I need to have a word about appropriate destinations for ladies of quality."

Lord Deloraine hammered on last evening for hours. Duties of a gentleman. Requirements of his son-in-law. Respect for his daughter. Does the man believe Marshall doesn't know these things? He may have been avoiding marriage, but a rapscallion he is not. Marshall's future father-in-law will be a continuous challenge. One thing is clear. He needs to find out more about who owns that red-wheeled cart with the Celtic knot painted on the trunk. The local pub, a good place to start. As soon as Marshall walks in the door, he's reminded once more that England is across the channel. At each table sits at least one man with his drink, with his friends, and with his knitting. A very different picture than an English pub.

Marshall takes a seat, places his hat on the bar, and chats up the barkeep. "I wonder if you can help me out?"

The half-bald man with a golden ring piercing his left ear wipes the bar in front of him. "What's that?"

"I'm looking for information on a cart with big red wheels."

"Yaup." He places his hand on his hip.

"Do you know it?"

"Yaup."

"Do you know where I can find the owner?"

He pulls on the earlobe without a ring. "Yaup."

"Well?"

The barkeep shrugs his shoulders and moves down to the other end of the pub.

"Won't get much more from him." Marshall turns to the voice at his side. It belongs to a short, middle-aged man. It's hard to see in the dim light of the pub.

"And you are?"

The man swallows a mouthful of ale, puts down his knitting, and offers his hand. "Emile Colins, at your service."

"And what service are you offering, Mr. Colins?"

"You were askin' information about the red-wheeled cart, were you not?"

"Yes. You know of this cart?"

"I might."

Marshall gets it. "And what is the cost of your clarification on this?"

"Show me what you're offerin.'"

Marshall isn't sure the man can be trusted, but at this point he's got nothing else so he drops a guinea coin on the bar. Emile takes the coin and shoves it in his pocket.

Marshall waits while Emile follows with another swig of his ale and picks up his knitting.

"Out with it."

"The red-wheeled cart." Emile clears his throat. "Belongs to The Fairy King."

"The what?" Marshall steps off the barstool and hovers above the little man.

Emile looks up and laughs. "Hold on, hold on. Don't be gettin' all full of angst. I'm just havin' a little fun."

"I'm not interested in a little fun. I need answers. Truthful answers, not some concoction of a Banbury tale."

Emile's laugh transitions to a smile. "I assure you, what I tell you is true. It does belong to The Fairy King."

Marshall has had enough. He grabs Emile by the collar. "I'll have my guinea back this instant."

"Hold on, hold on."

Chairs scraping the wooden floor, coupled with the low din of masculine voices, surround them. Marshall doesn't falter, doesn't flinch, his hold is firm.

Emile tugs on Marshall's hand to loosen the grip. It doesn't work. "Let me continue."

Marshall stares into Emile's round eyes, and then looks around at the men pinning them in. Their hands are free of yarn, free of drink, and fisted at their sides.

He lets go and steps back. "I'm waiting."

Emile straightens his clothes and repositions himself on the stool. "The Fairy King is a local florist and keeper of the largest nursery on the island."

"Interesting name for a nursery."

"He likes to think so." Emile finishes his ale and nods to the ear-pierced barkeep to fill it.

Marshall covers the glass with his hand. "Not until you finish telling me everything you know about this Fairy King."

"There's not much to tell. It's inspired from island tales of a fairy invasion where one fairy prince from across the sea stole away a beautiful local girl and took her to his kingdom. He left behind a magic pink lily to comfort her family. This is the Guernsey Lily. Some like to say the nursery owner is descended from this family. He grows almost all the lilies on the island."

"Not so." Another short, middle-aged man wearing a black beret sets himself up on the other side of Emile with his knitting and his ale.

Emile turns to see who it is. "Jacques!"

"Emile."

"What do you want?"

"To tell the man the truth, of course."

"The truth? I told him the truth."

"But not all the truth."

"The truth is the truth."

"Yes, but there is your truth and there is *the* truth."

Marshall rolls his eyes to the ceiling. He can't hear any more. "Stop. Just stop. I'll not listen to this fustian any longer." He focuses his attention on Jacques. "What exactly is it that Emile, here, neglected to tell me?"

"I can't tell you that."

"And why not?"

Jacques pats the bar with his hand and looks around.

"Oh, for goodness' sake." Marshall sifts out another guinea coin and drops it on the bar.

Jacques picks it up and blows on it before depositing it into his breast pocket. "If you insist."

Emile shoves Jacques so that he almost falls off the stool.

"I've had about enough of this." Marshall repositions himself between the two men. "Go on with it." Jacques clears his throat and leans forward to see what Emile is doing. Marshall blocks his view. "Here." Marshall points to his chest. "I'm the one you need to be speaking with. Now out with it."

"Fairy blood."

"What?"

"He didn't tell you about the fairy blood."

Marshall's chest begins to boil from the inside out. His head is set to explode. "I've heard enough. It's clear the two of you are wits to let."

"Hold on, now. Hold on." Jacques raises his hands to stop Marshall from leaving. "Let me finish."

Emile pipes up behind him. "You never learn, Jacques, you never learn."

Marshall turns around and sees Emile shaking his head in unison with the click, click, click of his needles. "Look. I don't know what the two of you are on about." Marshall looks from one and then the other. "But you better get to the point, before I make you both sorry you ever met me."

"Don't say I didn't warn you." It's starting to look like Emile is the type who always needs to have the last word. Marshall doesn't care who has the last word as long as one of them starts making better use of their words.

Jacques picks up his knitting and begins the cycle again. "I shouldn't be telling you this, and I wouldn't if I didn't need the coin."

"You've got the coin so get on with it, man."

"Emile left out what happened after the fairy prince took his bride back to his kingdom."

Click, click, click, click, click. The rhythm, mesmerizing.

"Well? Are you going to tell me or what?"

Jacques stops his knitting and gulps a swig of his ale. "They all wanted brides."

Marshall speaks into his glass and downs half his ale. "Of course they did."

Jacques's clickety-clicks continue, and Marshall watches the man's fingers while he relates the rest. "So the fairy soldiers invaded the island and killed all the local men. They took the beautiful Guernsey women for their own, married them, tended the fields, and started living here. It's why Guernsey men are shorter than average." Jacques surveys the room and then leans around Marshall to nod at Emile. He lowers his voice to a whisper. "And why the local witches no longer need broomsticks to fly."

"I'm sorry, witches? What does this have to do with the fairies?" Marshall regrets the question as soon as it leaves his mouth.

"Because they inherited invisible wings."

"I've heard enough. You expect me to believe this balderdash?"

"Told you. Too much." Emile shakes his head. "Too much."

A complete waste. A waste of time, a waste of money. He'll not get anything useful from this bunch. He'll send Ozanne. Maybe a local will be taken more serious.

Delia can't wait to get in the carriage and go. Her plans today do not include anyone else. One day of selfish indulgence. Maybe a new pair of Guernsey hose. She deserves it and no one is awake to stop her. She settles into the back and covers her lap with the blanket. No one will be pleased when they learn she's gone, and without her maid. Delia doesn't care. So few days left of freedom.

The hum in Delia's head won't stop. Engagement party anguish continues to twist and twine its way into every manner of distress. Each minute, each thought, each memory. They all can reach only one conclusion. Marshall doesn't want to marry her. Why else would he have left her side minutes after the announcement? Why else would he avoid her? Her father, the enforcer. That's what happened. He forces everyone. He forced Mel. He forced her. He's forcing Marshall.

Delia signals the driver to stop. She looks out the window while he opens the door and lets down the stairs. The moment she steps out, the girl across the path pulls her attention. The girl's full head of golden hair pours down her back in tresses of curly waves held in place with a pink ribbon. She spins around, and Delia recognizes her the minute she sees the pink nerine positioned above her ear.

"Lily?"

The girl curtsies. "Hello, my lady. Beautiful day it is, yes?"

Delia can't speak. Her eyes are glued to the golden brilliance.

"Are you all right?" Lily walks closer and touches Delia's arm. "My lady?"

"Yes, of course." Delia steps back. "I've never seen your hair before. I mean, not like this. The color is beautiful. I've not seen blonde this shade before."

Lily's smile slices her face with a half-moon sliver, not unlike the vision of a wicked mermaid Delia read about once in one of her mother's forbidden books. Delia shivers, shakes her head, and makes a conscious effort to focus on Lily's eyes when she speaks. "Papa calls it the color of the morning sun. I'm not allowed to wear it down at work." Lily's petite form, tiny voice, big hair, and chatterbox conversation mesmerize her. "Queenie would send me straight home with strict instructions not to return until it was put back together."

Delia stomps a foot once to try to break the intensity she feels while her attention wanders around the conversation. "I'm sorry. Queenie?"

The half-moon sliver returns to its quiet, new moon phase. "We call Mrs. Colins Queenie at Sausmarez. You know, the housekeeper?"

"Ah, yes. Mrs. Colins. She's very petite also."

"All the Guernsey ladies are. Haven't you noticed?" Lily circles her arm halfway around the market square showcasing all the residents of St. Peter Port.

Delia follows the imaginary line drawn in the air. Lily removes the pink nerine from her hair and hands it to Delia. "For you."

Delia takes it and twirls the stem between her finger tips. "It's very pretty." She inhales deep to enjoy the floral aroma. "Do you always wear pink?"

Lily takes the flower and starts positioning it over Delia's left ear. "It's my color." Lily steps back. "There." She looks around. "Did you travel here alone? I don't see your maid."

"No. I mean, yes. Yes, I'm alone. Promise you won't tell. I needed some time to myself."

Lily's smile appears again, and she links her arm into Delia's. "Very well. I shall walk with you down the lane. Who could I tell anyway?" Lily's soft voice starts getting softer and softer. Delia's legs are heavy. The merchant tables are on each side of them, tunneling her to the ocean. At least it sounds like an ocean. Lily's chatter stops. Delia's eyes are tired. She never should have come without her maid. She's alone. Where's Lily? Her legs are weak. She sinks. Someone lifts her up. Someone strong. Someone masculine.

Marshall watches a young girl link arms with Delia and guide her down the street. Lily is it? The servant girl from their engagement party? He can't tell for sure. She looks different. He walks a short distance behind so he can keep a close eye without losing them. He stops when they stop. Moves when they move. He slips behind a vendor's table when he's almost directly behind them. Something is wrong with Delia. Lily is panicking. At least it looks like she's panicking. Delia stumbles and reaches out to steady herself. Lily tries to hold her up but can't. He doesn't wait any longer. He steps out into the open and catches Delia before she falls to the ground. He immediately lifts her up and cradles her in his arms. He looks around for Lily. She's gone. He looks down into the sensational blue of Delia's eyes. Ice-blue eyes but warm eyes. Her head leans against his shoulder.

"What happened?"

"I'm not sure, but I think you fainted."

Delia looks around, groggy and confused. "Where did you come from?"

He can't help himself. He teases her. "The same place you did."

Delia squirms to remove herself from his embrace. "What?"

Marshall helps her stand and steady herself. She swipes the front of her dress to straighten the wrinkles and looks up at him. "Wait. You're the driver?"

He removes his hat and bows. "At your service, my lady."

"I don't understand. Why would you do this?"

He can't tell if she's angry, surprised, or afraid. Maybe a bit of all three. He takes her hand and presses it between his arm and side. "Come, let's walk and I'll explain." He bends forward to look at her from the front. "If you're up to it, that is."

"Of course I'm up to it."

She's mad. He shouldn't have teased her. "I only meant to show my concern."

Delia's countenance softens and the rosy color of her cheeks returns. They begin their trek back toward the carriage. "So. Are you going to tell me why you've inserted yourself as my driver?"

"I'm sorry to have deceived you. I was out riding, and I saw your intention to go out alone and given what I've recently learned, I switched with the coachman. I wanted to be there for you. Only if needed. For protection."

More color brightens her face. Wisps of her hair have come loose from her fall, and the ocean breeze tangles them in a frame around her face. He catches himself, wondering how these coral and copper locks would look flowing down past her shoulders. Delia's question stops him from going further.

"Protection from what? Papa hired those men."

"Yes, I know. But we still don't know who tried to seal us in Dehus Dolman or who took you."

Delia places her hand on her stomach. "With all that's happened, I hadn't thought about it for a few days now. Do you really think someone intends me harm?"

"I don't know, but I don't intend to give them another chance."

"What have you learned?"

"Nothing of significance. I've tasked Ozanne to see what he can find out."

Delia squeezes in closer to his side. The carriage is just ahead. He slows their pace. He wants to enjoy her company longer. Instead of taking her to the carriage, he guides her to the nearest cafe. He sits her down and orders a pot of tea be served with biscuits. "Now tell me about the young lady who was with you. Lily, is it?" He takes a seat across from her.

"Yes, Lily. You don't think she did anything?" He watches Delia pour their tea. She hands him his cup first. Her hands are steady. That's good. He takes a sip. Hot liquid burns the tip of his tongue. "Maybe." He sets the cup down so it can cool.

"She's only fifteen years old at most." Delia blows at the edge of her cup before she sips. She shakes her head. "I don't believe it."

"You wouldn't believe what the townsmen at the local pub told me either."

"Tell me." Her eyes are bright and excited.

"Best not." Marshall blows his tea this time before sipping. Much better.

"Come now. You can't leave me hanging."

"Truly, it's a bunch of nonsense. All island folklore."

"Now you must tell me."

Marshall can't resist her. "Fine. It starts with two fairies named Le Grand Colins and Le Petite Colins."

Delia starts to giggle. "No, really?"

"Really." He sips his tea and pays close attention to this woman sitting across the table from him. Easy to talk to. Easy to sit with. Easy to be with. In fact, he quite enjoys her company.

CHAPTER NINE

Delia removes her pelisse and throws it across the bed. She opens the small bag of chocolates Marshall gifted her. She drops one piece of the dark creaminess in her mouth. She sits on the sill of her window to watch the rain. Rhythmic drips and drops against the glass relax her. She sits back and closes her eyes. She wants to remember this day. Most of it at least. Marshall. Sweet and attentive Marshall. Not distant and absent Marshall. She enjoys listening to him talk about things that interest him. Things important to him. His silly stories of fairies and witches brings a chuckle to her lips. More because of the animated way he told it rather than the stories themselves. And Lily. Why did she leave her?

"Where have you been?" Mel's voice shatters her thoughts and the slamming door silences the rain.

"Out?" Delia flattens the remaining chocolate in her mouth and swallows. She slips the bag out of sight between herself and the window.

"Out where?"

"Does it matter?"

"What do you think? Of course, it matters. In case you haven't noticed, Dee, someone is trying to snatch you up."

"Don't be silly. That was Captain Mundo, and Papa paid him, remember? He wasn't even looking for me."

"Yes, I remember. What about the first time though? That was not Captain Mundo, if you'll recall."

"You've made your point, Mel. Stop. Please. Stop." This repeat conversation with Mel drains her consciousness. She massages her forehead in circular motions.

"I'll stop when you give me an explanation."

Delia takes a deep breath. "All right. First, I don't need to give you any explanation. However, because I choose to tell you, I will."

Mel crosses her arms in front of her chest and waits.

"Second, I'm not telling you anything until you settle yourself and stop acting like you're older and wiser and more experienced."

Mel huffs and slams her arms down her sides. She huffs her way across the floor, huffs herself into the chair in front of the window, and huffs once more while crossing her legs and folding her hands in her lap. "So?"

"I decided I needed some time alone." Delia raises her hand in a stiff reply to whatever was about to come out of Mel's mouth. "As it turns out, Marshall ended up joining me."

Mel nods her head. "Now that's what I want to hear." She moves over to the other side of the window sill and scoots closer to where Delia sits. "Details, my dear. I want details."

Delia shakes her head. She's not about to tell her Marshall posed as the driver. "We had a nice walk down High Street, and he bought me chocolates at a cafe not far from the Town Church."

"Mm. Chocolates. And what else?"

"Nothing else. We just talked."

"About?"

"Mel, I'm not about to tell you every little tidbit. But here, you may have one of my chocolates."

Mel looks in the tiny bag and sifts out a piece to pop in her mouth. "I accept, but I have some news for you."

"Oh?"

"I overheard Papa and the admiral talking earlier."

"Overheard? Don't you mean eavesdropping?"

"Dee, I would never eavesdrop."

Delia knows her sister too well to believe that. She decides to let it go. "And?"

Mel stops chewing for a minute and looks to the ceiling while adjusting the caramel with her tongue. "I was looking for you as soon as I heard."

"Heard what?"

"I heard loud voices from inside. They were arguing."

"And?"

"It's not eavesdropping if the entire conversation can be heard through the door without so much as a glass to your ear."

"Mel! Will you get to the point?"

"Yes. Right." Mel adjusts her skirt and repositions herself farther into the windowsill. "Papa wants him to take us to Scotland after you're married."

"Scotland? No." Delia's stomach twists and turns and tenses like a weathercock in a windstorm. "He can't. He knows what it's like there."

"I know, Dee. I know."

"I won't do it." Delia clutches her waist to settle the storm. "I'd rather stay a ruined spinster than be sent to Hermitage. How can Papa do this? We never go to Hermitage. It's a fortress, not a home."

"I know." Mel reaches over and pulls herself close to Delia. "It's haunted."

Mel rubs Delia's arm up and down in quick rhythm. "I'll figure out something. Don't worry."

Delia leans her head against her sister's shoulder. "No. Papa will never change his mind."

Mel's voice echoes in her ear. "Is Marshall here?"

"I don't know. Last I saw he was still with the carriage." Lethargy and hopelessness overwhelm Delia. There's nothing to be done.

Mel pushes Delia off her shoulder when she stands up. "Let's go find him. If anyone can help change the outcome, he can."

Delia looks up at her sister hovering over her. Mel doesn't understand. Delia isn't strong like Mel. Doesn't have the courage to run like Mel. Her father is a stubborn man. Once his mind is set, there is no changing it. "It's no use. You know how Papa is."

Mel pulls Delia with both arms until she's standing up. "Let's go. Now. We're going to see this fiancé of yours and make him prove his worth."

"I'm telling you Mel, he won't listen."

Mel walks Delia to the door and shoves her out. Right into one of the maids. The girl immediately stops and looks to the floor. "I'm so sorry, my lady. Please forgive me."

Delia lifts the girl's chin up from the floor. "No need for concern. Accidents happen. Daisy, isn't it?"

"Yes, ma'am."

"Are you hurt? Did I step on your toes?"

"No, ma'am. Apologies again, ma'am." Daisy curtsies and continues her hike down the hall, half running.

Mel stares at Daisy's retreat. Delia watches too. They look at each other. Mel speaks first. "Did you see her hair?"

"Her hair? Did you notice how young she is? She can't be more than thirteen."

"Dee, girls start in service younger than that. She must be an albino human."

"A what? Human's aren't albinos."

"What would you call her then? Her hair was as white as a winter moon and her eyes... Her eyes are the same color as the white tigers I saw in India."

"Mel!" Delia's jaw drops. "When were you so close to a tiger that you could see its eyes?"

"What? I told you. In India."

"Ugh. You're so ridiculous sometimes."

"I'm ridiculous? This coming from a woman who goes out alone after she's been abducted. Twice." Mel turns Delia in the direction of the stairs and shoves her down the hall.

"I'm telling you, Mel. Marshall can't change anything."

"Let's go find out."

"Why do you always have to have the last word?"

"I don't know what you're talking about."

"Liddesdale?" Marshall steps away from the billiard table. First the admiral is called away to meet with Deloraine, and now Ozanne returns from his assignment at the local pubs and is telling him this. Unbelievable. "You're sure?"

"Yes, sir. I spoke with multiple people. They all tell me the same thing."

"I knew something wasn't right with those two. I should have made them return my coin." Marshall picks up the chalk and twists it on the top of the cue stick then blows and twists again.

"The whole lot of them go to Liddesdale four times a year. With each change of the season, I'm told."

"Strange." Marshall bends across the pool table, takes aim, and shoots. It misses. He stands up and focuses his attention back on Ozanne. "And you say Mrs. Colins, the admiral's housekeeper, is related?"

"Yes, sir. She's married to The Fairy King's owner."

"I've heard enough. I believe it's time for a visit to The Fairy King." Marshall replaces the cue stick on the rack, dons his jacket and top hat, and steps out into the hall with Ozanne close behind.

"My lord, may we have a word?" A familiar female voice resonates behind him.

Marshall turns around to see the person who matches the voice. Lady Carmella. Delia is at her side. "Yes, of course." He directs Ozanne to continue on and prep his carriage. "Let's step in here." He motions for them to enter the tapestry room. Lady Carmella walks in first. Delia follows.

Before the door closes, Lady Carmella's words bite the air. "You have to call off the engagement."

"What?" Delia and Marshall's one word in unison echoes on the air.

Lady Carmella turns around and faces them both. "You have to stand up to him, or he'll be ruling your entire marriage."

Marshall closes the door shut behind them. "I'm sorry, to whom are we referring?" He already knows the answer.

"Papa, of course." Lady Carmella's matter-of-fact statements irk him. Being ordered by his future father-in-law is one thing. Having his own thoughts thrown back at him by his future sister-in-law is something entirely different. She probably doesn't even realize how much her actions resemble her father's.

Marshall stands with his hand still on the doorknob, watching the two of them. Lady Carmella lounges in one of two high-backed chairs next to the fireplace. Delia remains standing at his side, her eyes widen at her sister.

"Listen. The way I see it, you have two options. Continue on as things are and set the standard for your future, or take the lead and show Papa you're not having it."

Delia closes her eyes, takes a deep breath, and turns to Marshall. "I think she's right."

Marshall stares long and hard at Delia. He knows both he and Delia were against the idea of marriage before they were engaged. Now he's not so sure. He sees Lady Carmella from the corner of his eye, watching them both. He doesn't have time to discuss it. Ozanne is waiting for him. What can he say? The only thing he can at this point. "Agreed."

Delia watches Marshall leave the room. She waits to hear the door close, and then the clomp, clomp, clomp of his carriage. She flips around to her sister. Her voice roils. "What have you done?" Delia doesn't know whether to be happy or cry. It's full on war between emotions.

"What needed done, Dee." Mel props her feet up on a stool near the fireplace.

Delia stomps closer to where her sister is sitting, stands in front of her, and places her hands on her hips. "And you didn't see the need to discuss it with me?"

"I couldn't risk it."

"Risk it?" Delia plops herself down in the second high-backed chair and sits forward on the edge. "It's not your life we're talking about. It's mine." She slouches back. "I don't understand you. You force me to admit I have feelings for the man, and then expect me to let him go?"

"Dee, do you really want Papa controlling your lives? Controlling your marriage?"

"Of course not!" She sits up again, forward and straight. "I'm sure Daventry wouldn't let it go that far."

"Trust me, you have no idea. You didn't hear their discussion. Papa wants us locked up."

"And you shouldn't have either." Delia searches for something to throw at her sister. No pillows, nothing. A room covered in walls of tapestry should have at least one embroidered pillow. Delia settles for a scowl and a scuff of her boot against Mel's footstool instead. "How can I trust you? I don't think I even know you anymore."

"Pish!" Mel folds her arms across her chest. "I'm the same sister you've known all your life. You'll see."

Delia slouches back again. "I'm not like you, Mel." She props her feet on the edge of the same footstool. "I don't like playing games. I want people to be who they are and say what they mean." She intertwines her fingers in her lap and stares at the figures weaved on the walls.

"And you think I don't?"

Delia stares at her sister for a minute. "No. I don't think you do."

"How can you say that? The reason I left two years ago was precisely because I refuse to be what someone else wants me to be."

"That someone being Papa."

"Among others. And I think you'll agree, I always say what I mean."

"Not— "

The tapestry room door opens, the ladies jump up, and the butler walks in. "Apologies. I was not aware this room was occupied." He begins to close the door but not soon enough.

"That won't be necessary." A lavender clad gentleman sporting black, tasseled hessians enters the room. The purple peacock bows in front of them. "Ladies."

Mel's face burns red. Delia wants to scratch his eyes out of their sockets. Mel steps forward, but Delia grabs her hand to stop her. "Don't."

Mel jerks her hand from Delia's grip and glares at Captain Mundo. "What do you want? Come to snatch more innocent ladies?"

"Hmm." Captain Mundo stands in front of them with his hands behind his back and lips spread in a tight line across his face. "Not today."

The door opens again. Lord Deloraine enters. "Girls." He walks to a sidebar, pours two glasses, and hands one to the captain. "I hope you're being polite to our guest."

Delia answers first. "Of course." She can almost feel Mel boil next to her. She tries to take her hand again, but Mel resists. She glares at her sister and shakes her head.

Mel ignores her. "Papa, I refuse to be in the same room as this man."

Lord Deloraine takes one of the seats and motions for Captain Mundo to join him. "I'm sorry to hear that, my dear, for you will soon be in his presence for hours, if not days, depending on the winds."

"What do you mean?"

"I've hired him to take our family back to England. The admiral has been assigned elsewhere. Now that we've found you, and your sister will be married, I see no reason to continue on to France. We can all return together."

Another thin-lipped smile from Captain Mundo follows along with a silent toast. Delia wants to swipe the glass from his hand and empty its contents straight into his smiling, smug, sinful face.

Mel does it for her.

Marshall climbs to the top of the carriage next to Ozanne and reaches for the reins. "My lord?"

"I need to drive." He needs to clear his head. Consider what just happened. Focus on the task at hand. If he does nothing else, he'll find out who took Delia the first time. On his watch.

Ozanne relinquishes his hold and scoots over to make more room on the seat. Marshall slaps the reins and heads out the driveway. As soon as he turns the corner toward town, another coach pulls in with the Sausmarez seal. Must be the admiral. Ozanne doesn't attempt to make conversation, and he's glad for it. He needs to think. He needs to plan. He needs to decide. Decide how he's going to approach Deloraine. The man doesn't understand the meaning of the word no.

"There it is." Ozanne points to a building next to a large field with rows of colored flowers. The sign on the post reads, "The Fairy King." Marshall sets the brake, ties the reins, and hops down. Ozanne follows.

"No red-wheeled cart."

"Might have it parked in the back."

"Maybe."

They walk around the building and see a young girl carrying a basket of scarlet nerines. She doesn't look older than ten. Her pale skin is in strict contrast to her full head of titian-colored hair, tied in one loose lock hanging down her back. She sees them and heads in their direction.

"Can I help you?"

Marshall reaches out to offer assistance. "Let me help you." She rests the basket on her hip instead. "We're looking for Mr. Colins."

"Papa isn't here. My name is Rose. Can I assist you?"

Marshall looks at Ozanne and then back at Rose. "Is it true you'll be heading for Liddesdale soon?"

"Yes, sir. It is. We go back a few times a year."

"Do you now? I wonder if you could help me. I'm looking for safe passage for some artifacts I have from one of my digs."

"Your digs?"

"Yes, I'm an archaeologist. Do you know what that is?"

Rose lifts her shoulders, shakes her head, and restarts her trek toward the stone building. Marshall and Ozanne follow. "An archaeologist is someone who studies prehistoric people and their cultures."

Rose keeps walking. "I'm sorry, that is something you'll have to speak with Papa about." She sets the basket of flowers down on a stone bench and pulls a jar off the shelf. She opens it and sprinkles the powder all over them. It glistens. "Wait here a moment." Rose walks through a door leading to the main house. A variety of berets hang on coat hooks by the door. Marshall looks around the outer structure they're standing in. He pulls out his notepad and pencil and begins sketching the symbols carved in stones along the wall at different intervals. "Interesting."

Rose comes back out with ribbon and cloth and creates two small bouquets. She hands one to Marshall and one to Ozanne. "These are for you. Or you may give them to someone close to your heart."

"How much do I owe you?"

Rose smiles. "It's a gift."

"I insist. I must give you something." The last thing Marshall wants is to be accused of taking advantage.

"No. Papa always leaves a gift for recompense."

Marshall tries once more to refuse the flowers.

Rose will not take them back. "No, no, no. It's not allowed. You must take them."

Marshall looks at Rose and Ozanne and the nerines in his hand. "As you wish, young maiden. I accept your gift, but you must tell me what that powder was that you sprinkled on top."

"Plant food, of course."

"Right." Marshall replaces his notepad and pencil in his pocket before asking one more question. "Rose, my friend and I would enjoy a walk around the fields surrounding your house. What do you think?"

Rose looks behind her where the fields are located and shrugs. "I guess so. Maybe Papa will return by the time you come back around."

"Thank you." Marshall tips his hat, and she curtsies and smiles. Rose picks up her basket and skips back down the walk to the lined patches of multi-colored nerines.

Marshall walks through a stone archway leading to the fields in the back. He stops to look in all directions before deciding which way to go. His stride is fast. Ozanne struggles to keep up. It must be here. Somewhere. He changes course and there it is. The indentations that form a stone spiral. "As I suspected."

"What is that?"

"It's druid. Definitely druid. We can go now." Marshall heads back to the cart with the same force.

"Don't you want to talk to Mr. Colins?"

"I've seen all I need to for now. We need to get back so I can compare my notes to some reference books."

They reach the carriage. Marshall directs Ozanne to take the driver's seat. Ozanne lays his flowers down on the seat. Marshall picks them up and adds them to his own bouquet. "These need tossed. For all we know that powder could be poison."

Marshall steps into the carriage and Ozanne hits the road at a steady pace. Marshall tosses the flowers out the window halfway down the road. He leans his head back and closes his eyes. What did Rose mean about leaving flowers for recompense? Recompense for what?

Marshall sits up and pulls out his notepad to flip through the pages of his sketches of the symbols. They're all common and familiar to druidism. One symbol on the wall plagues him. It doesn't belong. He's seen the bent arrow and crescent before, but he can't place where. One thing he does know. Its meaning. Death.

CHAPTER TEN

"We may be going to France after all. Maybe India. Your father's in an uproar." Lady Deloraine enters the drawing room of Sausmarez Manor. Her paces across the wooden floor echo with each clip and each clop. "He's been in the library all morning with Daventry."

Delia focuses on each stitch of the handkerchief she's embroidering. Down, pull. Up, pull. She's not focusing on the squeamish turmoil happening in her stomach each time her mother mentions his name. Down, pull. Up, pull. She's not focusing on the tears threatening to fall. Not one bit. Down, pull. Up, pull. Not even the tremble hijacking her hands.

Mel's loud yawn from the direction of the settee switches the focus of her mother's tirade. Lady Deloraine points her finger at Mel. "I blame you for this. It has your workings all over it."

"My workings?"

"Yes, your workings. Delia would never go against her father's wishes. Take your feet off the furniture, child."

"Are you sure about that, Mama?" Mel sits up and brushes the ecru fabric where her feet were.

"Delia?" Lady Deloraine stops and clicks her tongue twice. "Have you nothing to say on the matter?"

Delia inhales deeply and tries to compose an appropriate response. Down, pull. Up, pull.

Mel comes to her rescue. "What do you want her to say? I refuse to allow Papa to do to her what he did to me."

"Did to you? What are you on about, child? Your father did nothing to you. You left, remember?"

"Yes. I do. I remember very clearly being shipped off to India with another one of Papa's minions. You know they call him the 'Enforcer?'"

"Listen to this nonsense, will you?" Lady Deloraine's eyes burrow deep into Delia with each word of the question. She refuses to look up. Her breath is tight in her chest. Her heart beats a fast rhythm. She exhales a deep breath. Down, pull. Up, pull.

"You were never shipped off to India, my girl."

"Oh? Have you asked him?"

"I didn't have to ask him. He told me." Lady Deloraine turns her back to the conversation, applying her attention to the view through the window instead.

"What exactly did he tell you?"

Lady Deloraine's voice softens, but is still harsh and pointed. "Exactly what happened."

"Do tell. I must hear this." Mel lifts her chin and folds her arms.

"You know full well he enlisted the help of a highly sophisticated lady to chaperone you to India so that you may have the opportunity for the best match possible, under the circumstances. There are plenty nabobs over there with the East India Company." She takes a seat next to Mel on the settee.

"Really, Mama? That's what he told you? And of course, you believe him."

"See? There it is. Always difficult. Always obstinate. There was no choice left for you after you ran away with that-that footman. Mr. Clockson." Lady Deloraine shakes her head and clucks twice.

"His name was *Cookson*, Mama. *Cookson*."

"You brought shame on the family. What chance would your sister have? Tell me this, will you?"

"What I will tell you, is this. Not everything was as you believe."

"Not everything, indeed. You know he's going to sue for breach of contract."

Down, pull. Up, pull. Tiny x's blur in the fabric. Threat has become reality. Tears begin to pour down Delia's face. Everyone needs to shut up and stop making decisions for her. Stop trying to protect. Stop trying to control. Tremors in her hands engage in a surge war with her insides. She tosses her needlework to the floor, stands up, and splays her hands down to her sides to gain control of all the emotion raging through her veins. "Enough! I've heard enough."

Lady Deloraine nods her head and scowls at Mel. "See how your influence affects her?"

Delia stomps her foot. "Mama. I am perfectly capable of my own reactions. I don't need you, Papa, or Mel to influence me."

"How can you say such things? I would never try to influence you. I know you to be capable of making rational decisions. Unlike your sister."

"Good. Then you will have no more issues with my decision to call off the engagement."

Lady Deloraine slaps open her fan and begins the fan dance. "I'll not be the one with issues come next week."

"What do you mean?"

The fan slaps shut. "We'll be sailing to France. Or India. Wherever your father's notion dictates we must go to wait out the scandal."

"Scandal? It's hardly a scandal." Mel's voice is still piqued.

Lady Deloraine's fan flips open. Slower oscillations ensue. "What else would you call it? He's already instructed me to make the necessary preparations. Already informed the admiral."

"I'm not going." Mel's argument is lost on Delia. One word is all she hears. *Scandal.* How is this happening? How can scandal be attached to her? Maybe they didn't think this break up through. She wipes the tears from each cheek before closing the door to the squabble. Maybe a visit with the horses in the stable will help put her life in perspective.

Marshall leans back in his chair. The admiral was good enough to allow him access to his library for researching his excavations. The least he can do now is follow through and figure out who's after Delia and what The Fairy King florist has to do with it. Marshall squints and rubs his eyes to refocus and clear the blur of reading small print. He stretches his arms above his head.

Deloraine's reaction was as expected. Marshall is not looking forward to the lawsuit. But now he's unattached. That's a good thing. Maybe. Truth be told, he's unsure how he feels about it. He was starting to get used to the idea of marriage. God knows he's attracted to the chit. It's what got him leg-shackled to begin with.

Marshall looks around the library walls filled with books. The admiral has a good selection of reference books. He returns his attention to his last selection. A very old journal. He can't find the name of the author. The book is ancient. Marshall carefully scans each page and flips it over. Journal entries date back to A.D. 968 and some earlier. It reads like the authors were Christian monks. How it remains intact is a wonder. A symbol etched in the margin draws his attention. He flips the pages of his notepad to compare the shape. It's exact. Even the vines twirling around it. Same as the red-wheeled cart. He flips back to where the journal entry starts and begins reading. The more he reads, the more sickness infiltrates through him, infecting his pores and numbing his senses. Human sacrifice is common throughout ancient history. But this. This is too close to now. Four women. Daughters of the King. A Fairy King. One for each season, pure, untouched. A white princess the color of the harvest moon, a bright golden princess the color of the morning sun, a light golden princess the color of the setting sun, a dark princess the color of the new moon at midnight.

His reading slows. Connections form. A description of the ritual makes his skin writhe. How could anyone do this to their daughters? Delia. It must be why they're after her. Something must have happened to one of their daughters. Why Delia? Lady Carmella must not be considered pure enough.

Marshall reads on. The monks believed it imperative that Christianity be installed on Guernsey. He can understand why. He takes a long, deep breath when he reads the last few sentences of the entry. This ritual takes place in years when there is a full moon during the winter solstice at the King's birthplace. All sacred rituals are held at the King's birthplace.

Marshall sits back in his chair. His head hurts, his stomach tenses. Liddesdale. It must be why they travel there. This "King" must be from Liddesdale. All this to ensure continued prosperity and perceived protections from pagan Gods. Sick. There is no other word for it. Demented? It doesn't matter. Marshall isn't going to allow them to get to Delia. Or anyone. This can't be permitted to continue. Time for another visit to The Fairy King. Identifying this man as soon as possible is crucial.

Marshall grabs his hat, puts on his gloves, and heads for the stables. As soon as he turns the corner, he sees her. Standing with her back to him. Leaning against his horse with the side of her head against the Arabian's thick, black coat. Crying. The Fairy King can wait as long as she's with him. He reaches out to touch Delia's sleeve. "My lady, is there anything I can do?"

Delia turns to face him and quickly wipes her tears with her hands. He presents her with his handkerchief. Her ungloved fingers touch his. She smiles through wet cheeks. "I'm sorry. I was just inside a moment ago working with my needlepoint. I hadn't planned on coming out here." She wipes each eye while muffling sniffles and laughs together. "I am not loose."

He joins her in this small amount of merriment, recalling the moment in the tomb where she first provided him with this piece of enlightenment. "Don't worry. At this point in our relationship, ungloved hands are the least of our predicaments."

Delia folds his handkerchief and hands it back to him. "Thank you."

He stops her. "No, you may keep it." There it is again. Uncontrollable urges. Marshall wants to take her in his arms and kiss her until there are no more left.

He watches her try to place his handkerchief in her pocket. She doesn't have a pocket. She stuffs it on the inside of her sleeve at the wrist. Aladdin nudges her arm and she begins caressing the horse's forehead, muzzle, and forelock. Even his horse can't get enough of her. "Can we still call what we have a relationship? Mama is furious. She said Papa is going to sue you for breach of contract. Tell me it isn't true."

"Not to worry. I'll work things out. I promise." He'll pay the price for breaking the contract. Anything for her. He lifts her chin to face him. He looks into her eyes and he can't help himself. Every instinct urges him to kiss her. But he holds back. Lord Deloraine's already burning fire doesn't need any more flame. Blasted marriage contracts. "I know what you need. What we both need."

"What's that?"

Marshall strokes his stallion's neck. "Aladdin will put you right."

"Aladdin?"

"From Antoine Galland's One Thousand and One Nights."

"Oh. I've not read him."

"Fellow archaeologist. I'll loan you the book, if you like."

Delia nuzzles against Aladdin, running her fingers through the course, blond hair of his mane and continuing along the dark black velvet of his coat. Every fiber in Marshall's being is screaming. He wants to trade places with his horse! He does the only thing he can think of instead. "Do you want to ride him?"

"They don't have ladies' saddles. I already checked. Since the admiral's family is away, all their saddles went with them."

"Who needs a saddle?" Now he really wants to trade places with his horse. "Have you ever ridden bareback?"

"Of course not! I told you, I'm not—"

"Loose. I know. Are you sure you don't want to try?" He watches her conflict. She's struggling with the idea.

"Come." He makes the decision for her. He takes her hand, grabs the bridle hanging on the side of the door, and opens the stall. In no time, Aladdin is ready to go. Marshall grabs Delia's hand again and walks them both to the grasslands behind the stable, hidden from view.

"I'm not sure this is a good idea."

"Sure it is." He's not letting her change her mind. He folds his hands and lowers them so he can give her a leg up and into her seat on Aladdin. "Scoot forward just a little." The smile on her face tells him exactly what he already knows. He walks them to the side of the fence where he can mount up and join her on the horse's back.

"What are you doing?"

"Riding." Before she can say anything else, he nudges a soft kick to Aladdin's side to move them forward at a slow pace. "Relax. Let your legs hang. Don't tense up. Let me do the guiding." Marshall keeps Delia close to his chest and pinned between his forearms.

"I feel like I'm going to fall off."

"You're not. Grab hold of Aladdin's mane to steady yourself."

As soon as she does, she leans back into him. He feels the tension release in her body. Her hair tickles his cheek. He whispers in her ear, "This is one time where you absolutely should be loose."

Delia looks over her shoulder at him. Her smile gives him permission. He kisses her cheek at the corner of her lips, almost on her mouth. One last time. "How about a little faster?"

Delia tightens one glove and then the other. Her heptagon reticule dangles from her wrist.

Mel's voice shakes her. "Dee, it's time to go."

Delia swallows. "I can't believe I'm going to say this." The lump in her throat won't go down. "I want to stay."

Mel joins her at the window of the room she's occupied during her stay at Sausmarez. "I know."

Delia concentrates on the garden below. Also the stables. So much has happened in the few weeks she's been in Guernsey. Mel's hand on hers draws her attention back to the present and the sister once thought lost. "Let's be thankful we're not being forced to go to Hermitage."

Mel is right. She can't shake the melancholy gripping the center of her being. Will she ever see him again?

"Girls!" Lady Deloraine scrambles into the room. "It's time. The carriage is waiting in the front." She claps her hands together twice. "Come, come! Be quick. We need to reach the docks in time."

Mel holds Delia in place while turning around to address her mother. "Give us a minute? Papa hired him, remember?"

"Yes, yes. Of course, your father hired him. We are, however, at the mercy of the tides you know. Unless you wish to be stuck here another day, which I do not, you best make haste."

Delia swallows again. "Mama, please." Her mouth is dry, her tongue sticks to the roof of her mouth when she speaks. She swallows and clears her throat. "I need only a moment."

Lady Deloraine gives them both a sideways eye roll. "What is the matter with you? One would think you'd be pleased to be returning to London."

Mel squeezes Delia's hand. "Don't you mean Scotland?"

"Of course, Scotland. London is first. What do you think, child?"

Mel puffs out the air between her teeth. "Of course it is. We'll be down in an instant."

"Instant, I'm sure. I'll be waiting for you in the coach. I expect you to follow only minutes behind." She turns to leave but stops at the door for one last remark. "Don't make me send for you."

"As you wish." Mel rushes to the door to close it. It's not like Mel to be so docile. She pulls Delia to the chair and forces her to sit. "Tell me what you want."

"What do you mean?"

"It's been a week since your engagement was broken. First you don't want to be married, now you're like a lost pup in search of its master."

"Mel, what would you have me do?"

"Are you going to sit there and let Papa control your every move?"

"You're the one who put us here. You tell me what should be done next."

Mel rolls her eyes and places her hands on her hips. "Ay yi yi! The two of you. Do you want the man?"

Mel's question sparks an immediate reaction. Her heart beats yes. Her mind says yes. Every part of her being screams yes. It was settled the instant he kissed her cheek during their ride on Aladdin.

"Dee?"

Tears break the barrier holding them back. One tear after another rolls down Delia's cheeks. Mel kneels in front of her. "I'll take that as a yes." Mel's smiling face almost looks amused.

Delia's words break through between sobs. "Oh, Mel. What am I going to do now?"

Mel wipes her sister's tears and pats her hands. "Leave that to me. I'll fix this."

Yes. She's definitely enjoying this.

Marshall opens Aladdin's stall and the horse immediately nuzzles his nose against him. "Looking for this?" Marshall pulls out a carrot and offers it, then walks him out, fastens him between two posts and begins brushing. Long, careful strokes across the thick fur coat of his back, hip, shoulder, and down. Aladdin's midnight color shines more with each stroke. Spending time with his horse brings him much needed calm. And comfort. Marshall didn't sleep all night. Every time he visits The Fairy King, it's owner is absent. It's beginning to feel intentional. And Delia. He can't shake the ride he shared with her. He's running out of reasons to be at Sausmarez.

"How goes it, old man?"

The familiar voice brings a smile to his face. "Freddie!" Marshall lays the brush on Aladdin's back and turns around to greet his friend. "I'm well," he lies. "What brings you this way?"

"I stopped at Havilland's. They said you're boarding your horse here?"

"Right. Havilland's stalls are full. I make use of the admiral's library most days anyway. And with Delia...er, was with Delia."

"Something I heard about that. A broken engagement. It's true, then?"

Marshall inhales deep. "Yes, I'm afraid it is."

Freddie leans against an empty stall. "I'm guessing you're not as well as you'd like everyone to believe. Otherwise, you'd be letting the stable boys take care of the grooming."

Marshall picks up the brush again. "Is it that obvious?"

"Only to those who've known you as long as I have. I saw the parade of carriages leaving when I rode up. Want to talk about it?"

Marshall switches brushes and begins working on Aladdin's mane and tail. He's not interested in rehashing the sequence of events.

"I'll take that as a no."

Marshall stops brushing. Freddie means well. "It had to be done. I'll not live under a dictatorship." He puts the brushes away, grabs the horse pick, and puts his weight against Aladdin to force him to shift his weight so he can clean the horse's hoof.

"Do you love her?"

Marshall puts Aladdin's hoof down, stands up, and leans against his flank. Freddie's question perplexes him. He's never been in love. He's never contemplated marriage. Until Delia. His work is all-consuming. The idea of marriage to one woman forever, intimidating. It's different with Delia. Everything has been different from the moment they met. Her interest in the prehistoric. It's what prompted him to take her to that blasted dolmen to begin with. Most females wouldn't go anywhere near a dig site, let alone a tomb.

"Is it that difficult of a question?" Freddie's words snap him back to the present.

"No. Not anymore." He does love her. He's loved her from the instant his lips touched hers.

"What are you going to do?"

Marshall knows exactly what he's going to do. He finishes cleaning each one of Aladdin's hooves, saddles him up, and mounts.

"Shall I join you?"

"Only if you can keep up. I've got a ship to catch."

He urges Aladdin on toward St. Peter Port. Aladdin doesn't disappoint. Marshall takes a shortcut. He has to make it on time.

He reaches the docks and searches each carriage, each ship. He'll know Captain Mundo. Will he recognize his men? Found them. He leaves Aladdin tied to a post and makes his way along the path to the *HMS Wolfe*. The salty sea air smells of dead fish.

"Don't forget these." Freddie jogs up beside him and hands him a bouquet of scarlet nerines. More Guernsey lilies.

"What?" His gut shouts to toss them into the sea. Confusion on Freddie's face stalls him.

"I got them from a young miss across the way. I thought they might help, all considering."

Marshall doesn't have time for this. He picks up his pace. He needs to reach the ship before they set sail.

Freddie keeps up. "I only thought since the fairy prince from England will be taking his lady, he might wish to offer these to her mama in exchange for the lady. A little Guernsey folklore never hurts, don't you know. Softens them up a bit."

Frustration reigns Marshall. Any more fairy princes and Guernsey folklore and it's *boom!* He's at the brink, set to detonate. He snatches the flowers from Freddie and steps into a run. Pedestrians separate to allow Marshall to pass. Sailors along the marina prepare their ships, anchors drawn, and sails ready to catch the wind. His heart thunders when he reaches the *Wolfe*. The boarding plank is still installed. He runs up it. Lord Deloraine and Captain Mundo are in conversation on deck. Mel and her mother are standing along the rail. Lord Deloraine holds up his hand to stop the conversation and heads in Marshall's direction.

"What it is?"

"I've changed my mind." Marshall can almost taste the brine in the air.

"I can assure you I'm not interested. You've made your intentions quite clear. You'll be hearing from my solicitor."

Marshall examines the flowers in his hand. The hollowed abyss called his stomach expands. No amount of flowers will be able to repair or soften anything. He puts them behind his back. He has no intention of giving them to her anyway. He must see her. One last time. "Please, sir. Allow me to at least say good bye."

Lord Deloraine doesn't take his eyes off Marshall when he yells for his daughter. "Mel! Get your sister out here."

Lady Carmella walks closer to where they're standing. "Papa, I told you Delia is feeling ill. She's locked herself in her cabin."

Lord Deloraine turns his attention to her. "I said bring your sister on deck so we can get this over with."

She scrapes her toe into the floor boards of the wooden deck. "I can't."

"What do you mean you can't?"

"Delia's not on board."

"Not on board? What are you talking about?" Lady Carmella takes a step back and her father takes a step forward. "Stop fooling around. Let Daventry say his peace before the tide takes us out."

She stands straight. Her height equals her father's. "I said. I can't. Delia isn't on board."

"Where the devil is she?" He whirls around to call for his wife. "Loraine!"

Lady Deloraine scurries to where they're standing. "What is it, dear?"

"We're getting off." Lord Deloraine motions for Captain Mundo to join them. "Change of plans."

"What's that now?"

"Delia's not on the ship. Secure the anchor. Gather some men. We need to find her."

"Papa, it's not necessary. I know where she's going." Lady Carmella faces Marshall. "She went back to Sausmarez. To find you."

A speck of joy creeps into the darkness he thought he might have to live with for the rest of his life.

Lord Deloraine bellows at his daughter. "I'll deal with you later. Go with your mother to the carriage and wait till we get back."

"But, Papa. She's safe. She's not alone."

"What do you mean?"

"I arranged for her to meet up with Lily and Daisy from Sausmarez. She's meeting them in front of the Town Church."

Marshall's abyss just became bottomless. He hands the flowers back to Freddie. "Wait. She's with both of them?"

Lady Carmella squeezes her lips and folds her arms across her chest. Lord Deloraine grabs his daughter's upper arm and pulls her close to his face. "Carmella Rutledge. Tell me. All of it. Now."

"Papa, you're hurting me." She struggles to free herself.

Captain Mundo steps close between them and lightly tries to separate Lord Deloraine's grip. "Sir, might I suggest we not wait any longer since we know her direction and who she's with? We need to catch up with her and bring her back before the tide rolls out."

Lord Deloraine pierces the captain with Enforcer heat and shoots the same pointed expression back at his daughter. He shoves her in Captain Mundo's direction. "Take her to the carriage with her mother. Have one of your men guard her. Do. Not. Let her out of sight."

"No! Papa, I want to come."

"Not a chance in Hades."

"Papa, please." Captain Mundo steps in front of Lady Carmella, forcing her to walk backwards toward the carriage where Lady Deloraine is waiting. She pushes him back. No surprise at his response. Captain Mundo lifts her up and bends her over his shoulder, carrying her the rest of the way. Marshall keeps an eye on them from a distance. He wants to help her, but the only woman who has his complete and full attention at the moment is Delia.

Lord Deloraine redirects his attention back to Marshall. "Take Mundo with you and bring her back here."

"It's not necessary for Captain Mundo to come. Freddie and I can manage."

"It wasn't a question. If you run into trouble, Captain Mundo is a good asset to have with you."

"I don't doubt it. I assure you, Freddie and I will have it under control." Marshall isn't about to let a jackanapes like Captain Mundo near Delia. Not after what he did to her. He doesn't care if her father paid him to do it.

"Let me put it to you another way. Take Captain Mundo or any chance you have with my daughter is off the table." Marshall has had enough of Deloraine's take-charge titan temper. He'll find a way around it as soon as Delia is safe.

Captain Mundo returns, wiping blood from his lip with the back of his hand.

"I see my daughter finally hit her mark."

Marshall bites the inside of his cheeks to keep his grin from splashing across his face. Captain Mundo walks past Lord Deloraine and speaks directly to Marshall. "Let's go."

CHAPTER ELEVEN

Delia sees Lily and Daisy waiting for her in front of the Town Church. Right where Mel said they would be. How did Mel get so clever? Sneaking off the *Wolfe* while cargo was offloaded almost cost her the egg and sausage she had for breakfast. Her stomach continues its loops and coils. She's still shaking from the scheme of it. Lily and Daisy greet her and curtsy in unison as soon as they see her. Both are wearing bonnets. Good for them. Daisy's albino coloring will no doubt draw attention.

"I'm so happy to see you again, Lily. I was worried something happened to you when you disappeared at the market. Where did you run off to?"

"I'm so sorry, my lady." Lily's eyes bore holes into the ground in front of her. "There was a man who jumped out from behind one of the vendor's tables. Papa always tells us not to wait when faced with danger. Run and don't look back, he says. I shouldn't have left you. I panicked."

Delia has no choice but to console her. Sorrow plays the chords of Delia's heart. She looks at Daisy, who isn't speaking at all. Her heart wrenches for these girls. So young. So innocent. "It's all right. It turns out the man you are talking about was Lord Daventry. He saw I was faint and stepped up to help. I'm sorry he frightened you."

Lily pulls out a bouquet of pink nerines from her bag and hands them to Delia. "Here. I offer you these for recompense."

Golden sprinkles scattered on the petals of each blossom glisten in the sun. Even the stem glistens.

"They're beautiful." Delia sniffs their floral scent. "How do you keep them so fresh and glowing?"

"Plant food, of course."

"Do you know what's in it?"

Lily shakes her head. "Papa makes it. You can ask him. He's waiting across the street to give us a ride back."

"Wonderful. All the walking I've done today has made me tired." Delia follows the girls across the street to a blue cart with big red wheels. A short man wearing a black beret hops off to help each one into the back. "Thank you for taking us back to Sausmarez." A vague memory presses forward. Delia yawns.

"Pleasure's mine, dearie. All mine."

Marshall, Captain Mundo, and Freddie trot down High Street in the direction of the Town Church. Marshall tightens Aladdin's reins. Traffic makes him anxious. The captain and Freddie struggle with their horses to keep them from nipping each other. "This will not do." Marshall sees an opening and urges Aladdin ahead so he can maneuver through a gap and into open road. The others follow. In minutes they reach the Town Church. Marshall scans the walkways surrounding it. No sign of Delia. No sign of Lily. A splotch of pink flowers on the ground across the street catches his line of sight.

Freddie aligns his horse on one side of him. Captain Mundo on the other. "What is it?" Freddie's question drowns out all the activity going on around them.

"I'm not sure." Marshall rides over and dismounts. Freddie and the captain follow. Marshall picks up one flower. He looks around for Delia. For Lily. He starts asking each person who passes by if they've seen a red-wheeled cart, the driver, a lady with two maids. Nothing. He asks if anyone has seen The Fairy King and they stare. Freddie stops him. "Hold up, Daventry. Hold up."

Marshall refocuses his attention on his friend. He sees Captain Mundo standing in the distance, holding the lead for his horse. "We have to find her. You don't understand. They're going to kill her."

"Who's going to kill her? The maids?"

"No! The Fairy King. I have to get to her."

"Stop. Slow down." Freddie holds him firm on each shoulder. Marshall shakes himself loose. He sprints back to Aladdin, but before he can climb up, two strong arms wrap themselves around his chest and squeeze. Captain Mundo.

Only it's not Captain Mundo. Marshall looks to one side and then the other. Freddie and the captain are both ensnared with a similar strong-arm tactic. In three beats, Captain Mundo flips his attacker over his shoulder and knocks him out. Marshall can't breathe. Can't budge. Where did these three Guernsey men come from? One looks familiar. The pub? Captain Mundo comes to his aid. "Go. Get her. I'll take care of things here."

As soon as Marshall is free, he runs a straight line to Aladdin. He glances back. Freddie and the captain have things under control. He looks ahead and goes the only place he can think they would take her. Vale Castle. He heads for the Braye. The place he found her before. Before he knew her the way he does now. Before he knew...he loved her. His instincts prove true. Pink flowers dot the trail along the way. Good girl.

He spurs Aladdin to run harder, faster. He must reach them. Branches snap underfoot. Branches snap overhead. He ducks to miss. Leaves crackling beside him makes him look. Loud barks and agitated breaths sync together. "You." How does this animal know? Instinct? It doesn't matter. Marshall encourages the rogue mutt to stay with him. "Good boy." He'll take all the help he can get. In any form. As long as he gets to her before it's too late.

Two beasts and one man move forward toward a common goal. The goal is almost in reach. There it is! The red-wheeled cart. The golden knot with green vines on the rear panel. No mistake. Each gallop closer, the more in focus the picture in front of him becomes. Two girls support a third. Delia. Lily too. His ally beside him barks. The little man wearing a black beret turns to look. He urges the cart to go faster. They're almost to the Braye. Marshall's got them. He knows it. They have nowhere to go. Or do they? The little man drives them straight into the water. What is he doing? They'll drown. Aladdin gallops high-speed. Marshall watches the little man and his two daughters jump in the water leaving Delia behind. They unhitch their horses from the cart. Water flows over the sides. Why isn't Delia sitting up? Rogue pulls ahead barking and growling and dives in after them. Marshall must get to Delia before she goes under. He reaches the edge of the Braye, jumps off his horse, and dives in. He climbs inside the cart, grabs Delia's hands, and raises her up to a sitting position so her head is above the water. He positions himself beside Delia and holds her against him. The water is at their chest. She's not moving. He leans close to see if she's breathing. Her breath grazes the side of his face. He pats her cheek on each side. "Delia? Wake up, love. Please wake up. I can't lose you now." It's fear that fills the abyss now. "I have so many things I need to tell you. I love you." He presses his lips to hers.

She opens her eyes and smiles. Her words are soft and sweet. "I love you too."

One large splash follows one large animal hopping from the driver's seat, over their heads, and into the water pooling around them. An onslaught of happy dog kisses slathers them both.

"Easy boy." No keeping him back. "I don't think there's any doubt as to how this one feels."

Delia giggles and wraps her arms around the dog's neck and scratches behind his ears. "I always knew you were a softy. You're such a good boy. You need a name."

Marshall stands up. The mutt hops out and starts swimming to shore. They need to get to shore too. Marshall holds his hand out to help Delia up. She loses her balance and falls against him. He helps her hold onto the side while he gets out. The current is strong. He wades to the opposite side, allowing the cart to block the strength of the water. Delia climbs out into his arms and he helps her get her footing. Together they wade back to shore. Marshall gives her a leg up on Aladdin and then climbs up behind her. Rogue mutt is nowhere to be found. Typical.

Delia is ice cold. Shivers break out against his chest. "We need to get you out of these wet clothes."

She snuggles back farther against him and giggles. "This isn't the first time you suggested I remove my clothes. Is this going to be a regular occurrence?"

He smiles and kisses the side of her head near her temple. "I certainly hope so."

Sailing home to London aboard the *HMS Wolfe*, Delia watches cerulean blue waves in all directions. Peaceful, calm, enchanting waves. The smell of the sea air this far out invigorates her pores. Or is it the man standing next to her, holding her firm and steady with the motion of the sea? "Are you sure they won't find me?"

"I'm sure. Your father and I have made arrangements. Ozanne will handle the legal side in Guernsey along with the admiral when he returns. We've already sent word to the magistrate in Liddesdale."

"What if it's not enough?"

"Believe me. Your father is not a man to be trifled with. We'll get them."

Delia blows out a deep breath. "You know Mel told me people call him the 'Enforcer.'"

"I've no doubt. This is one instance I'm glad of it."

Mel paces up and down the deck, wearing the same black, deplorable pants and cloak she wore when Delia first saw her on the island. It's good her mother and father are below deck. Their cross words are not what Delia needs right now.

Captain Mundo scans the horizon with his spyglass. What is he on the lookout for? She doesn't have to wait long to find out. A wild wind whistles through the sails.

"Take cover and hang on!" The entire ship rises high before sinking low.

Marshall wraps one arm around Delia and the other around the rail. He pushes her to the floor of the deck and shields her from the water that splashes over them.

Mel doesn't have time for cover. The force of the water crashing the deck drags her close to the edge. The entire scene unfolds in slow motion. Captain Mundo swoops down from his position at the wheel in true swashbuckler form just in time. Just in time to stop her from going overboard.

Soaked. Everyone on deck is soaked. Captain Mundo stands up and offers his hand to Mel. She refuses, pulls herself up, and starts wiping down the front of her wet, black clothing. He examines her from the top of her sopping wet hair to the bottom of her black hessian boots. He smiles his toothy grin before yelling out orders to his crew. He turns to Delia, Marshall, and Mel. "I'll need you to remain below until we reach land."

Mel shakes her head. "Not a chance. I can't be below deck."

"Listen. You'll do as you're told or I'll throw you over my shoulder and take you there myself." He pulls out his spyglass and searches the horizon again.

Mel folds her arms and stomps one foot. "No!"

What's gotten into her? "Mel, you must. We'll sit with you."

"Not for all the tea in England!"

Captain Mundo inserts the spyglass back into his pocket. "I don't need all the tea in England." He hoofs it closer to Mel. "What I do need is to make sure my passengers are safe." He picks her up, throws her flailing body over his shoulder, and marches her down the stairs to the dining area. The line of passengers follow.

Mel's feet touch the ground. One swing. One miss.

Captain Mundo shakes his head, smiles, and heads for the door. "One day you and I might actually—"

"Never." Mel slams herself down in the chair and rests her head on her hand.

Marshall looks at Mel and then at Delia. "I'm going to change into dry clothes." He kisses her cheek. "I won't be long. You might want to— "

"I know. Get out of these wet clothes."

"Exactly."

Delia sits down across from her sister. She reaches out to touch her hands. "Em, what is it?"

"What do you think it is? I'm going back to the very place I swore I would never return to. I can't do it."

"You know I couldn't stand it if you left me again."

"Dee, you're going to be married. And I'm happy for you, I am, but I have to figure out what's next for me."

"But Mel. You're older, more experienced, wiser. Things will be different. It's been two years. Papa told everyone you were in India. No one knows except us about Cookson."

Mel jumps back in her seat. A tail appears on the other side of the table next to Mel, along with a whining howl and smacking lips. "Where did you come from?"

Delia looks under the table. "That mongrel saved me. Twice."

Mel scrubs the back of his ears while his face rests in her lap. "I remember you. You're the one that joined our dinner party, aren't you?" Mel lifts the dog's head in line with her face.

"He looks like he might be an Irish Wolfhound. A dog the likes of him deserves a name, don't you think?"

"Marshall calls him Rogue Mutt. Rogue for short."

Mel leans down and kisses the top of his head. "Rogue suits you." Mel touches her forehead to his. "You're a good boy, aren't you? Yes, you are." She takes the dog's head between her hands again to look him in the eyes. "Hey Dee. Look. His left eye is brown and his right is green. How cute, yes?"

"Let me see." Delia walks around the table to stand behind her sister. "Hmm. Odd. Just like Captain Mundo."

"What?"

"Captain Mundo has the same eye colors. One brown, one green."

"No. Really? I hadn't noticed."

Delia shoves her sister's shoulder. "Probably because you're always facing his backside."

"Not nice. Not nice at all." Mel stands up and pretends to go after Delia and chase her around the table.

Rogue howls in response. Mel calms him. "Whoa. Whoa. We're just playing." He barks one more time before turning around and leaving the room. "Typical male. Always has to have the last word."

"Not unlike someone else I know."

"I don't know what you mean."

Marshall fidgets, alternating from one foot to the other. He sticks his finger between his neck and collar to loosen it. His cravat is too tight around his neck. He steps back, tiptoes up and down, and waits.

Sweat beads on his forehead. St. George's is hot. He looks behind him at the vicar. No sweat there. He pulls out his timepiece. Almost ten fifteen. The ceremony is scheduled for ten. He waits.

Marshall glances around the chapel at his family and friends sitting in the pews. Some are smiling, some are staring, some are yawning. He waits.

Floral-colored ribbons are positioned delicately at the end of the pews. No flowers. They agreed it best, given their past. Not yet, anyway.

He looks over at Freddie standing next to him. "What is taking Delia so long?"

Freddie pats him on the shoulder. "Shouldn't be too much longer. Ladies and their perfectionism, don't you know."

"Perfectionism?"

"What else would you call needing everything to be just so?"

Organ music permeates the rafters. Marshall stands at attention and immediately searches the back of the aisle. The doors open, everyone turns. Lady Carmella walks down first and takes her position opposite them. The melody changes and the doors open again. Perfectionism barely describes Delia at this moment.

Apricot curls wind wild around her head leaving one, long and lone, resting over her shoulder. Her silk tulle veil hangs the length of her body on each side, meshing with the chiffon fabric of her dress. Gold lace embroidered in the bodice of her gown frames the emerald pendant hanging low between her cleavage. His breath is snatched from his throat.

His sight is drawn to each curve when she walks, each touch when she steps, each breath from her lips. Each move bringing her closer to his side. Each move taking more of his breath. Each move... She's here. Standing with him.

He reaches out to take her hand. He wants to kiss it, but holds back. Instead, he folds her arm with his and presses it to his side. He can't take his eyes off the beauty next to him. Beauty soon to be his. Forever.

"I pronounce that they be man and wife together..."

The minute the words are said Delia's heart skips and races, sending shots of something new to the well of her stomach. Is it joy? Whirls of thoughts, anxieties, prayers, and happiness invade every part of her. His warm hand holding hers soothes her nerves. She's never letting go. The vicar continues his blessings and prayers. Delia peeks over at the man she will now call husband. Marshall is watching her too. He squeezes her hand in response. The organ explodes in unison with her heart. The ceremony is over. Mel kisses her. Mr. Lukis congratulates them. All the guests file two at a time to the exit, and Marshall guides her out. Out into a flurry of white rice, well wishes, and teary eyes.

Marshall swoops her up and carries her to a waiting yellow barouche with four white horses. They're not seated two seconds and he wraps his arm around her. "How does it feel to be the new Marchioness of Daventry?" Marshall's question surprises her. How can she express the conglomerate of feelings threatening to seize her?

Marshall doesn't wait for her to answer. "Never mind." He squishes her close and kisses her firm on the mouth. A kiss more different than any of his kisses before. Soft and gentle. Lingering and steady. Sweet and divine. It's at this moment she realizes. This man in her arms belongs to her. Forever.

EPILOGUE

The Indian sun toasts the air into hot waves. Delia opens her eyes and sees Marshall's empty spot on the mattress beside her. She runs her arm across his pillow and recalls the evening they shared in each other's embrace. Every night with Marshall is a new, exciting, heart-pounding experience. She sits up on the edge of the bed. The air inside the tent is as hot as it is outside. She looks around their makeshift home full of fine china, wooden furniture, and floors carpeted with oriental rugs. The only difference from home are the four tent walls.

She washes her face, gets dressed, and brushes her hair. The door flaps open and Marshall walks in. "Good morning, love." He kisses the top of her head and hands her an envelope. "The courier from Bombay just arrived."

Delia recognizes the handwriting. "Mel."

"I knew you would want to read it right away."

Delia hurries to open it. "It's been months since I've had news."

Marshall steps out and comes back in with a tray of tea and biscuits. She reads each line blurting out sentences and phrases. "And Mel's being sent for a season to stay with my cousin, Ariana."

"Is that a good thing?"

"I don't know. They're the storm chasers I told you about."

"Ah yes, of course. I look forward to meeting them. Very interesting conversation to be had, I'm sure. And your parents? Any news?"

Delia reaches for a biscuit and takes a bite. "She doesn't say much. Only that Papa is his usual forceful self."

"Are you almost ready?"

Delia looks up from the letter. Marshall is standing at the door, packed for a day of exploration and excavation.

Delia dips the last bite of her biscuit into her tea, pops it in her mouth, and downs the remaining liquid from her cup. "Let's go. I can't wait to see what you have to show me today."

Marshall hands her a sack, takes her by the hand to lead her out of the tent, and across the green grass in front of massive stone carved structures built into the side of the mountains. "Bhangarh Fort. It's over two hundred years old."

Delia scours the land, shielding her eyes with her hand. "Fascinating." The entire area is green and swarming with wildlife. Beige and black monkeys are her favorite troublemakers. Snakes and spiders, no.

Marshall lights a lantern by the entrance and holds it high so they can see where they're going. He steps in first.

Delia grabs hold of his waist and scrunches close behind him. "Explain to me again, how this is better than Hermitage?"

Marshall takes her hand and walks her through the ruins. He stops at the archway to a dark room and sets the lantern on the floor at their feet. "For one." He kisses the tips of her fingers. "India is far enough away from England that you should be safe from that blasted druid cult until they're all rounded up."

"Hmm." Delia raises on her tiptoes and kisses her husband's cheek. "My hero."

"And two..." Marshall kisses the inside of her wrist, sending zings of chills down her spine.

She wraps her arms around her husband's neck and pulls his head down close to hers so she can see deep into his dark, chocolate-brown eyes. Eyes she makes a habit of getting lost in.

"...hauntings, here, are only said to happen at night."

Delia pulls back a smidgen. "Wait. You brought me to excavate *haunted* ruins?"

Marshall's firm grip on her hips keeps her in place. "Hold on. It's only a legend. And no. I brought you here to look for the tomb of a princess."

"Tomb?"

"You do know you married an archaeologist."

"Yes, but does it always have to involve tombs? Why can't we excavate somewhere more... I don't know...civilized?"

"Hmm." Marshall kisses the lobe of her ear. "What about an ancient university?"

"Yes! Much better. When can we leave?"

THE END.

IREANNE CHAMBERS

If you enjoyed reading Folly at Sausmarez Manor, please consider giving it a review.

Read more from the Majestic Estates Series by stepping back a few years to 1798 and read Ariana's story in Storm Chasers of Wentworth Hall.

Books from **IreAnne Chambers**:

Majestic Estates Series:

Storm Chasers of Wentworth Hall.

Folly at Sausmarez Manor

Mystery at Harlaxton House

Wolfe of Toddington Peaks

Regency's British Empire Series:

Aphrodite Mine

Isle of My Man

Aliens of Extraordinary Ability Series:

Nightingale Song

Bollywood Bargain

Seasons Bliss Series:

Countess who Kissed a Count

One Man and a Babe

Find all books by IreAnne at:

www.IreAnneChambers.com

Join the **The Cozy News** for New Releases.

ABOUT THE AUTHOR

IreAnne Chambers' books contain the spirit and tone of the traditional Regency with the promise of mystery, adventure, and mishap intermixed to create a happy-ever-after with plenty of fun and surprises along the way.

She looked to her Scottish and Irish heritage and discovered the name Eireann (Erin). Eire means Ireland in Gaelic and IreAnne was born.

IreAnne also enjoys writing poetry and song lyrics, but her love for the Regency romances of Jane Austen, filled with dashing heroes and feisty heroines, spurs her desire to write Fun, Cozy, Historicals, And Then Some...

As novelist and Nobel Prize winner Toni Morrison said, "If there's a book you really want to read, but it hasn't been written yet, then you must write it." IreAnne does just that.

Follow IreAnne here:
BookBub
Goodreads
Instagram
Facebook
Pinterest
Twitter

Don't miss out!

Visit the website below and you can sign up to receive emails whenever IreAnne Chambers publishes a new book. There's no charge and no obligation.

https://books2read.com/r/B-A-FKKH-VWNW

BOOKS 2 READ

Connecting independent readers to independent writers.

www.ingramcontent.com/pod-product-compliance
Lightning Source LLC
Chambersburg PA
CBHW030322160726
47992CB00005B/2122